I0548923

Also by Seth Edgarde

Hart Island
The Devil Speaks Hungarian

BLOOD SUNRISE

SETH EDGARDE

BLACKBIRD BOOKS

NEW YORK • LOS ANGELES

A Blackbird Original, July 2013

Copyright © 2013 by Seth Edgarde
All rights reserved.

Manufactured in the United States of America.

The events and characters depicted in this book are fictional.

Cataloging-in-Publication Data

Edgarde, Seth.
Blood sunrise / Seth Edgarde.
p. cm.
1. College students—Fiction. 2. Alcoholism—Fiction.
3. Crime—Fiction. 4. Brown University—Fiction. I. Title.
PS3605.D4564 B56 2013 813′.54—dc22 2013943427

Blackbird Books
www.bbirdbooks.com
email us at editor@bbirdbooks.com

ISBN 978-1-61053-023-1

First Edition

10 9 8 7 6 5 4 3 2 1

To my parents, Charles and Rebecca,
who gave me an education in more ways than one.

BLOOD
SUNRISE

1

My eyes open into the dark blue gloaming of dawn. It's the cold that wakes me. I'm outside somewhere, in a park, and the chill has gotten into my bones. I can only see out of one eye; the other, the left one, is just a blur. I must've lost a contact lens somewhere. The sunlight is speckling off the water down the berm where I'm sitting on a park bench. My eyes, both of them, hurt.

My head feels full, and the sunlight makes me squint, even though it isn't strong. *Hungover.* But I can't remember just how. It hurts to even consider trying to retrace my steps. I'll figure it out later. I always do. For now, it'll be enough of an effort just to figure out where I am and get myself back to campus.

The air is moist, and, combined with the touch of early spring frost, it makes me shiver. I have on a sweater, but my legs are bare, poking out from under my powder blue skirt. Dressed up . . . Yeah, I remember now . . . Last night, the dean's spring cocktail party . . . I was going to talk to him, try to con him into letting me graduate. I have more than enough credits—I've been at Brown almost five years—but they're spread across three majors, and I'm short in each one.

Yeah, the dean . . . Jensen . . . He likes pretty girls, so I wore a skirt and stockings, hoping he'd be a soft touch, but I never even got to talk to him. I remember *that* now too. And those stockings . . . Yeah, I had on pantyhose, had to go to CVS to buy them, squeezed into them behind the dumpster in the back of the store. I remember, because they were a size too small, and they were tight, and I was afraid someone was going to see me, even though the bin hid me and it only took a minute to put them on and straighten myself out. Sitting on the park bench, now in the cold, I can feel my feet still tucked into my loafer pumps. But how the hell did I lose my pantyhose?!

I begin to get scared. *You're a drunk, Emily*, I tell myself. *A blackout drunk.* It's the first time I've admitted it to myself, but it gives me no relief. But it does make me finally exert that mental effort to figure out what had happened last night . . .

It was about six o'clock, and I was getting ready to head over to the party, and I asked my roommate if she was going. My roommate, Jill, that irritating blonde from California— *Northern* California, as she'd always remind me—I didn't particularly want her along, but I hate going into a social event alone. She said no; she was staying in to study—boy, on a Saturday night, you can't get more pathetic than that—but then again, she's probably happily asleep in a warm bed now.

Anyway, she was the one who stopped me, told me about Jensen, told me to wear a skirt, flash a little leg. "Don't worry, he won't hit on you. He's not like that. But look pretty and give him a big smile, and he might help you," she told me. *You don't stand a chance. You're a fuck-up and a loser* was what she meant. I could hear it in her voice. But she was right about Jensen. And now, here I was, twelve hours later, bare-legged in the park. But this wasn't Central Park, I wasn't Jane Fonda, and Robert Redford was nowhere to be seen. It was just some crummy park on the Narragansett, down river of Providence, and I was dead alone. Maybe my roommate was right about *me* too.

The sun has come up a little more, and it's beginning to get light. The park is actually pretty, and a fresh smell makes me inhale deeply. Oddly enough, it makes me remember, by contrast, the smell behind the CVS, and then the walk over to Weybossett Hill and the dean's house the night before. It was a big, yellow Colonial, and it had given me a twitch of envy from the plain, split-level I grew up in, back in Indiana.

When I walked in, the house was crowded. With all the fuss about my wardrobe, I had inadvertently made myself fashionably late. I talked to a guy I knew from my sophomore dorm—Steve somebody-or-other—who was surprised that I was still there. "Didn't you graduate?" he asked, innocently enough, but it made me feel awful. I was 23, and, frankly, graduation was nowhere in sight. "No, I switched majors, so it's taking me a little longer." *What a loser*, I thought to myself. I felt like going home and getting drunk, but I really needed to find Jensen. I had no idea what I was going to say. A shot of Southern Comfort—just one— would sure help. Problem was, it was a dry party—college kids and all. I suddenly felt old too. Time to reconnoiter. I went over to the bar for a cranberry juice.

"You look like you could use a *real* drink," said the bartender in a thick Rhode Island accent.

Jesus Christ! Does it show? "No," I said emphatically.

Then he smiled. "It's okay, I could use a stiff one myself."

I didn't want to, but I smiled and laughed a little. He was a townie, dark and good-looking, probably from Federal Hill or thereabouts. "Is that an offer?" I heard my voice ask, feeling myself abandon my better judgment just a little.

He looked at his watch. "I have a break at seven. Meet me back in the kitchen in five minutes."

He winked at me. It was so corny and old-school that I wanted to roll my eyes and tell him to get lost. But I wanted that drink, and he was cute, even if he was just a horny townie on the make. I'd get my shot, calm myself, and find Jensen. I had no choice. My dad was running out of tuition money.

A half hour later, we were making out in the pantry. I told him I had to go, and he told me in five minutes, took a swig, and handed me the bottle. It was vodka, Grey Goose, but it would do. At least it was the good stuff.

"Okay, five more minutes," I told him.

He was a surprisingly good kisser and knew enough not to grab me where I didn't want to be grabbed. At least not too soon.

When I looked down at my watch again, the hands were in the same place, and I realized my watch had stopped.

"What time is it?" I asked in a half-panic.

"I don't know, maybe eight."

Normally, I would have freaked, but the booze had taken over, and I just laughed. "Don't you have to go back on duty," I said to him, forgetting about Jensen altogether.

He shrugged his shoulders like Don Juan. "I'm just filling in for my cousin. Party's almost over anyway."

He went back to kissing my neck. We were on the floor, and his hand was on my hip, and I didn't care.

"Isn't *he* going to get in trouble?"

"Believe me, he'd understand. Besides, he owes me."

Good enough for me. I finished off the last of the Grey Goose. I looked at him, eyes as big as possible, "Got anything else to drink?"

He took my hand, got up, and pulled me along. "Come on, let's get out of here."

He had an old blue Caprice, and we stopped at a liquor store down on Wickenden, before heading out. "I know a nice quiet place down river a ways." He shouldn't have been driving, but then again, however drunk he was, I was worse. I was sure I'd had more to drink, and I was half his size.

When we got to the park, we sat alone in the car and kept drinking, keeping the high, building it even more. He'd bought beer for himself, and I finally got my bottle of Southern Comfort. I used the beer to wash it down.

"I have to go to the bathroom," I told him after a while.

I should have been scared to go out of the car alone, into an empty park, in the middle of the night, but I was never afraid of anything when I was drunk. The moon was waning, but there was enough light to see. I was looking for a good tree or a bush to go behind when I stumbled over the restroom. I was surprised to find Danny right behind me. He grabbed my ass, and I turned around and kissed him. I reached for the door and pushed on it to go into the ladies' room, but it was locked.

He pushed against me, pressing me into the locked door, and we kissed furiously. I reached over for the other door, the men's room, pulling myself away. "I really have to go," I told him. I could see in his eyes that he thought I meant *leave*. I looked him in the face. "I just mean I need to pee."

He grinned as I reached the other door, following me. This one opened, and he pushed me inside, touching my breasts and backing me up to the sinks. There was a row of them, white porcelain with space in between, and he grabbed my butt and hoisted me up so each cheek was sitting on the side lip of a pair of adjacent basins. It was surprisingly comfortable, and he worked his way in as I opened my legs. We kissed, and he moved, and I wasn't sure what would happen next, but I felt wild and free, but my bladder was so full, and there was something in the way. I stopped him.

"These damn pantyhose," I said, gently pushing him off and slipping down onto my feet.

I reached up and pulled them down, almost taking my underwear with them but making sure to keep them on. For now, at least. When they were down to my knees, I pulled myself back onto the sinks, took off my shoes, and pulled the pantyhose off completely, stuffing them in my purse.

"My mother told me never to take your hose off in front of a man," I announced.

He didn't seem to care. He came back in, this time pushing against my underwear, and I was suddenly glad I'd worn matching panties. I found myself still unsure, unsure of what was going to happen, of what I *wanted* to happen. Even drunk, sex was a big deal to me. There had only ever been two times before, both with the same person, a childhood friend named Steven Smith. Once the summer before college, in the lifeguard shack at the lake back in Bloomington, and the second time after he'd transferred to Brown when I was a sophomore.

Maybe it was thinking about Steven, or maybe my hometown, and my dad, and that tuition money, or maybe it was just my incredibly full bladder, but I decided to put on the brakes. I was just about to stop and speak, when Danny spoke first.

"I got to take a massive leak," he announced, pulling away, holding my shoulders.

The look on his face was so earnest, almost apologetic, that it made me want to keep kissing him. "Me too," I said, giving him permission.

So he went to the urinal, and I slipped back down into my shoes and went into the nearest stall. As I sat peeing, relief washing over me, hearing him pee too, I suddenly had to stop myself from laughing. It just *sounded* so funny, two people tinkling. Looking at the shadows in the moonlit bathroom, my amusement wore off. It was dark and mysterious, but I still wasn't scared. There was no toilet paper, which didn't help, but my underwear was already wet, and the urge to be touched overtook me again. I began to notice the smell.

We went back out into the park and over to the bench, where I'm sitting now, alone, in the morning light. I don't remember any more, and I know I'm not going to. My headache is even worse. The alcohol has mostly processed through my system now; I can feel it. I need water and I have to pee again.

I reach down to push myself up off the park bench, and I see my stockings . . . snagged on a splinter. Vision half-blurred, I follow it, pulled taut down underneath the bench. And there, right underneath me, visible between the slats, is Danny, dead, my pantyhose wrapped tight around his neck.

2

Stumbling off the bench, twisting around so as not to turn my back on Danny's contorted face, I fall on the ground, my neck and shoulders arching down the hill. I let out a few staccato sounds, quiet but filled with terror. In a craze, I move backwards, in a four-limbed spider-walk, struggling against the dew-wet grass to get away, until I am in a near-tumble down the incline, towards the Narragansett. I stop. "Get a hold of yourself, Emily," I say in a whisper. But my chest is heaving, and I start to cry.

I wipe my eyes on the sleeve of my sweater, temporarily displacing my one good lens, but it floats back in place before I have a chance to react. I sit on the ground catching my breath, until I look back over the crest and see his shock of black, curly hair. *I've got to get out of here.* I get to my feet and climb up and around the bench, cutting a wide berth and looking away from the sight underneath.

I want nothing more than to get out of that park as fast as possible, but I have to go to the bathroom so badly, I'm ready to wet myself. In fact, my backside is *already* wet.

Maybe I actually *did* wet myself. I reach around and feel the moisture on the back of my skirt. No, it's just dew from the grass, although it feels soaked-in in a way that's odd.

Heading to the bathroom, I see the car on the left. No use to me now. The door to the ladies' room is still locked. *Of course.* I use the men's room, stupidly picking the same stall. Still no toilet paper. Then I notice that my underwear is wet—not just on my butt but between my legs too. I look down in the toilet and see the big wad that's oozed out of me. It takes me a moment to realize. *Semen.* So we did have sex after all. But I don't remember it. And I don't know if I let him or he forced me.

I finish, waddle out of the stall with my underpants at mid-thigh, and pad them with paper towels before pulling them back up. I take off my sweater and tie it around my waist to hide the stain. It's still cold, and I'm glad I'm wearing a long sleeve shirt.

Exiting the bathroom, I try to figure out where the main road is. I still don't know where I am. Then I realize that I've forgotten my purse. My purse! My cell phone! GPS! But did I remember to bring it? No. I took it out and left it on my dresser. Damn.

But still, I have to find that purse. And my missing contact lens too, if possible. I don't want to leave anything of mine behind, but if I can't find it, the police might not either. And even if they do, it's probably not on his . . . body, so they'd have no reason to believe it belonged to his killer. But still, I have a heavy prescription—minus 7.25 with a bad astigmatism—distinctive, but not exactly a fingerprint.

I shudder when I realize that I have to go back over to the bench to find it. I can't bear to see him there, and I have to stop for a moment. What the hell happened? What am I going to do? Flee the scene of a crime? Call the police?

I don't know what happened. Was I raped? Did I kill him? Maybe. *Probably.* Who else? And why would they leave me alive. I think about the caretaker. It was just that once, but it happened.

I walk back over and see my purse scrunched under his hip. Grimacing, I pull it out managing to not touch him in the process. It's small and doesn't hold much, but it's my favorite, decorated with Indian beads, and I'm glad to find it. There's dirt embedded in the beads, and I know that I'll have to get rid of it when I get back to school.

I search around for my missing lens, inspecting but not touching the body, before finally giving up. Then I realize I only have two dollars to get home. Not enough. Girding myself, I finally touch him, pushing my hand into his pocket, looking for money. Nothing in the front. I roll him over, still not finding the lens but getting his wallet and a ten dollar bill from his back pocket.

I notice the car one more time on my way out and take a minute to wipe my prints off the door and handle and anywhere else I might have touched, inside and out. By the time I find my way out of the park and back to Boston Neck Road, I know that I'm somewhere near Jamestown, not too far from U.R.I. I find a bus stop. I wait for almost half an hour before one shows.

"Does this go to Providence?"

The driver, a stern New England type, shakes his head. "You want the 14. Should be around in five, ten minutes. Other side of the street."

"Thanks." I smile at him, but I don't mean it, and he knows it.

Another ten or fifteen minutes and the bus I want stops. It's a woman driver this time. She's fat but not jolly. I don't bother to fake a smile this time, and she takes off before I have a chance to get my seat, nearly sending me to the ground.

There are only two other people on the bus: A guy sitting in the back about my age or maybe a couple of years younger who looks about as hungover as I am and an old woman with a very wrinkled face and no teeth, sitting up front. I walk down halfway between the two and pick a seat on the driver's side.

Not wanting to ruin my sweater, I untie it and take it from around my waist before sitting. I feel disgusting even as fatigue overtakes me. But I can't sleep. All I can do is think, think that maybe I've killed someone. My mind drifts to the caretaker . . .

I went to a prep school in the middle of Indiana, about a thousand students, grades 4-12. It was expensive, hard to get into, and sent lots of kids to places like Brown and other Ivies. I played field hockey, took oboe lessons, and edited the school paper. I also won the national Latin prize and graduated valedictorian, all of which was good enough to get me into Brown and the four other Ivies I applied to plus another half dozen schools that parents like my mother drool over.

I also liked to drink. It started with a few parties in ninth grade—mostly beer and wine. I told myself I was just having fun, blowing off steam, that it was nothing. Everyone did it. It was only a few beers.

By eleventh grade, I'd started in on the hard liquor, vodka, gin, and what became my favorite, Southern Comfort. I started drinking alone, breaking into my dad's stash. He hardly drank, himself (most of it had been my mother's, and she left it when they got divorced). But pretty soon, even he would notice the bottles going down on their own. I had to figure out another way to get booze. I was underage, and I looked it.

Then one day in the fall of my senior year, when I was coming back in from field hockey practice, I knocked over a garbage can. It was my turn to carry the team's equipment bag, and I was struggling with it—big, heavy, and unwieldy, especially for a 5'6", 120 pound girl, who was all of seventeen. So when I went for the keys to the storage room, slinging the bag down to the ground, the can and its contents went with it. I heard the clink even before I saw them—empty booze bottles, three or four of them— sprawled on the floor.

Looking up, still holding the key, I noticed that the door to the storage room was ajar. The supply room, downstairs, out by the athletic fields, was the domain of Willie, the caretaker. Rumor was that he drank. And those empty bottles seemed to be chiming in with an opinion of their own on the matter. With the door open, he was probably nearby, or maybe even inside. A moment later, I saw his feet.

I didn't know him, except in passing. I don't think any of the kids did. He was quiet, did his job, and kept to himself, only occasionally flashing shots of impatience or anger when someone abused a piece of equipment or chewed up a field beyond what was reasonable. He never smiled and seemed a bit aloof, but nobody really even noticed him. Just another invisible part of the background at Rutherford-Bloomington Prep.

I looked up at him, guilty, but unable to stop my eyes from darting back down to the green bottle that used to hold a full fifth of Tanqueray gin. "Cute" had gotten me out of things before—like cleaning up a mess I'd just made—but this was different. When I looked back up, my eyes were pleading and made contact with his. He didn't say anything at all, but I could tell that he saw it.

He took the equipment bag with one hand, swept it into the other, and dropped it inside the storage room. Then he bent down and shoved the garbage, bottles and all, back into the can, waving me off as I tried to help. There was empathy in his movements and actions, and I stayed where I was for a moment, unsure, until I got up and left.

I was back again the next day. It was my job for the week, but for once I was glad. The door was ajar again, and I poked my head in with the oversized bag.

"Hi," I said, smiling.

He took the bag and put it aside, looking at me for an instant and then away.

"Thanks," I said, still standing in the doorway, awkward for a second.

He grunted back a primitive sort of acknowledgement, and I stood waiting for more. I took in the room. It was big and messy and smelled like dust. All sorts of junk was in there, the accumulation of decades of athletes and activities: Catcher's mitts of players who were now bankers, professors, and fathers. Music stands for sopranos, basses, and trumpeters, whose lips and voices now said and did things that gave no hint of their musical past. I wanted to stay, drink myself silly, sitting on his ratty couch, not giving a damn about school or grades or anything, but no invitation was coming, so I left.

It went on like that all week, with my "Thanks" and his grunts, but I noticed that every day when I came in from practice, he was there. Finally, that Friday, I saw a bottle of gin peeking out from the side of the couch, like a shy invitation.

"I'm really thirsty," I said, looking right at the bottle.

"There's a water fountain outside," he said, waving his arm and not looking up.

I shook my head, sick of the game. "So it's going to be like that," I said, entering the room and heading straight for the gin. I picked it up, wiped the open top with the inside of my forearm, and drank right from the bottle. I plopped down on the couch and handed him the bottle. He drank without wiping.

"Can you get some Southern Comfort?" I asked, looking over at him.

Back on the bus, I look out over the Rhode Island landscape. It's pretty, spring life coming back from the straw-yellow winter ground. The ocean smell and sparkle reminds me that Narragansett Bay is just off to the right, and the breeze coming across through the open window from the other side of the bus tells me it's warmed outside a bit. It's a pleasant sensation, sitting there in the bus, ocean breeze and March sunlight, but it's one I don't deserve.

Danny, the dead boy, the one I . . . the one I was with last night . . . he and his black curly hair won't let me enjoy this ride. But I can't think about him now. It's too much, and I'm too tired. So I go back to Willie the caretaker . . .

We sat there on his couch in the equipment room until the bottle of gin was done, and I walked home. I lived less than a mile from campus and liked being outside, so I never took the bus. And I'd learned to hold my liquor well enough by then to look sober on my walk and even get past my dad without arousing suspicion. He'd never guess that his straight-A perfect daughter was a hard-liquor drunk, using every bit of effort just to walk straight.

"You look tired, honey," he said when I came in.

"Yeah, I've been studying in the library for my AP Calculus exam."

It sounded so fake, I felt like laughing.

"Well there's meatloaf in the oven whenever you're hungry."

For a second he sounded like my mother. Well, not *my* mother, but *somebody's* mother.

"Thanks, Dad," I said, finally disappearing up the stairs.

It was too much, even for me—too much *booze* that is. I fell asleep in my clothes and didn't wake up until it was time to get up for school again. And I didn't go back down to the caretaker's room for almost two weeks after that. But when I did, he was glad to see me. It was my free period, just before AP English.

I guess absence really does make the heart grow fonder. I hadn't meant to, but I'd inadvertently played hard to get, and Willie liked having a drinking buddy, even if I was just a stupid, spoiled, rich girl.

I came down every day after that, except Wednesdays when I worked on the paper. I even managed to sneak over for a quick drink on Thursday mornings after orchestra practice.

We never talked much, and even then, it was mostly about what kinds of drinks we liked. It went on like that for weeks, and I still knew amazingly little about the man. But I didn't care. That room and that ratty couch with Willie and his stash of liquor were my escape, my valve to get away, lose control, and get wasted.

Sometime in the middle of January, just after Christmas break, I saw him in the hallway up where the classrooms were. I hadn't been down in a few days—busy working on the yearbook and studying for my last AP exam. He caught my eye, gave me a little signal, and I knew he had a bottle of Comfort for me. I didn't like that he'd come up looking for me, but I went down anyway. I was still recovering from Christmas with my mother, and I needed a drink.

He was acting strange from the minute I sat down, but I didn't care. I broke into the SoCo and took two big belts before handing it over. We had long since dispensed with wiping the top, and when he handed it back, I put it directly to my lips and took another long draw. By the time we were halfway through the bottle, I was feeling *very* relaxed.

I had forgotten all about my mother and her blond hair and pretty blue eyes. And her new boyfriend. *Hargrove*. What a ridiculous name! They were living together now. They both had tenure at IUPUI, the joint campus of Indiana and Purdue Universities in Indianapolis. It was all so cute.

I propped one leg up on the couch and turned to Willie. "You have any kids?"

But he didn't answer. He just stared at me. And then he put his hand on my knee. I bristled, pulled my leg away, and put my foot back on the floor. I don't think I blushed—I wasn't embarrassed or even afraid—but I felt like I'd been hit by a train.

Willie was repulsive. And old. I wasn't sure how old, but I was pretty sure he was even older than my dad. He was horseshoe bald, had a grimy beard, and was incredibly badly groomed. Gray-streaked reddish-brown hair was sprouting from everywhere but the top of his head. And there I was, sitting across from him, and he wanted me. I felt like throwing up.

I was pretty wasted at that point and got up to leave. I wasn't sure if I'd ever come back. I walked over to the door and turned, looking over to thank him for the drink, but he was right there, standing almost on top of me.

He reached out and squeezed my breast. I was so drunk, I hardly felt it, but I instinctively pushed his hand off. And then I slapped him. His head bobbed back, and I saw the anger and wanton desperation in his eyes. He came back in and grabbed me, pulling me in for a kiss, but I shoved him off. I was stronger than I looked—carrying that equipment bag and all—and I was absolutely fearless when I was drunk.

Grip broken, he stumbled back, and glancing to my side, I grabbed the first thing I saw, a garden awl, and, as he came back at me, I shoved it into his chest. He fell back over a stack of chairs and landed on the floor. I could see the red fanning out from under his shirt. I turned and left the room.

When I woke up the next morning, I was sure I'd killed him, but there was no announcement at school, though I did hear, a day or so later, that Willie was out "sick." I wasn't sure what that meant, and I didn't want to ask. It was all I could think about for the next several days.

Meanwhile, I'd caught a cold I couldn't shake, and I was having my period—heavy as usual. I felt awful. Somebody finally noticed. It was my history teacher, Mr. Casey. He told me I looked pale, and I told him I didn't feel well. I left class to go to the bathroom, and there, in the empty hall, coming at me was Willie. It was cold, and I was clutching myself for warmth, pulling my sweater in tight. I walked right past him and the bathroom, avoiding his eyes and saying nothing. But I could feel his glare.

The corner of my eye caught the edge of a white bandage peeking out from under the collar of his shirt. I clutched myself tighter and kept walking, passing a second bathroom and heading right for the school nurse. She called my dad, told him I was sick, and he came and picked me up.

I started crying in the car, and my dad got upset. I told him it was just my period, and he said, "Oh," in that uncomfortable way that men do, and he took me home and put me to bed. Lying there in my pajamas, I thought about how I stabbed Willie in the chest and almost killed him. I certainly *could* have killed him. But then again, he tried to rape me. He deserved it. Besides he didn't die. I'd just seen him, walking around, absolutely fine. So nothing to worry about. He certainly wasn't going to tell anyone.

But this time is different. This time, there's a body.

3

The bus stops at the Greyhound station downtown, and I get up, tie my sweater back around my waist, and head up the hill to campus. It takes about 25 minutes, and I'm flagging. I need some water and a couple of aspirin. And some sleep. I do my best to push the whole thing out of my mind.

It's about 8:15 when I finally get back to my dorm room. Incredibly, my roommate is exactly where I left her, sitting, cross-legged on her bed, books open, pencil in hand, studying.

"Hi," I say, forcing an incongruous smile to cover my shock.

She looks up with a knowing grin, and I see her eyes go down to my bare legs. "I see the stockings worked out okay."

"I didn't have time to get them," I lie.

"Well then I guess *no* stockings worked out okay."

I'm in no mood for her. I just want to take a shower, get into my pajamas, and go to sleep. And now here she is, eyes right on me in our tiny little room. I need to get undressed, but I don't want her to see the grass stains on my butt.

Or the wet. Although by now she certainly knows that I was with someone last night. I wish I had a single.

I think to go to the shower with my clothes, but in the end I wrap a towel around myself and pull my clothes off underneath. Losing my grip at the last minute, the towel falls, just in time for her to see me completely naked.

Picking it up and re-covering myself, we both catch a glimpse of my body. Dark, French-Canadian, like my dad.

"I'll be right back," I announce, for no particular reason.

Towel tight around me, I enter the bathroom. It's only a week until spring break. I've already got my ticket home. If I can just make it to Friday, just make it back home to Bloomington, I'll rest, reconnoiter, figure out what to do about school. It'll be okay.

In the shower, I wash myself, and *more* of *him* glops out of me. I feel queasy. But my feelings of guilt begin to dissipate. *If he did attack me, he got what he deserved.* I finish my shower and suddenly remember how thirsty I am. Wrapped back in my towel, I go over and drink directly from the sink. The water is cold, and I practically devour the spigot. Providence water tastes good, not like the bitter hard, lime infused water in Indiana.

Back in the room, I realize I don't have any aspirin, and I don't feel like asking Jill, even though I know she has some. I'm about to drop my towel on purpose this time and go for my pajamas, so tired I no longer care, when I notice someone else is in the room.

I still have my one contact lens in, and I see the figure of a guy standing over by my desk. Brown leather shoes, jeans, a nice shirt . . . It takes me a second.

"Tim! Hi!" I say, standing in my towel like an idiot.

It's Tim somebody-or-other from my astronomy class. I'm about to ask him what the hell he's doing in my room at 8:30 on a Sunday morning (in the nicest possible way, of course), when I remember: We have a class outing at 9:30, up at the observatory on the north end of campus. Solar flares. I'm so tired I could drop. I'd blow it off in a heartbeat, but it's required to pass the course. I'd promised Tim I would go with him. He's got a crush on me, and I didn't have the heart to say no. But now I'm glad—I can't afford to lose any credits at this point—even though all I want to do right now is sleep and clear my mind.

He's dressed like he's going on a date, and it makes me feel bad. There's nothing wrong with him; I'm just not interested. I'm sure Jill knows that I forgot, but I don't want Tim to find out.

I give him a cute little eyebrow wrinkle. "Sorry I'm running late. I'll be ready in like five minutes."

"Oh yeah, no problem," he says, heading for the door. I see his eyes check me out, and I feel the little bit of energy I have left waning.

Jill looks over at me, but I ignore her. I just want to get out of here and get this over with as soon as possible.

Underwear, bra, jeans, belt . . . No, no belt . . . And a top. I fumble through three or four of them before I find a plain white one with long sleeves that I like. I reach for my sweater and feel something on one of the buttons. It's my missing lens, dried hard and ruined, but I feel relieved. I decide against the sweater before taking my other lens out and putting on my glasses. I hardly ever wear them, but I'm out of fresh lenses.

I look at myself in the mirror. Still 5′6″. Now at least 125 pounds (I never quite lost that freshman ten). Brown hair, brown eyes. Average, average, average. And now, a pair of thick, black, rectangular, wire-rimmed glasses. I can't for the life of me see what there is to have a crush on. But clean and dry and able to see out of both eyes, I definitely feel better.

I look at my watch. 8:37. Time to go.

It doesn't take me long to realize that this *is* a date. He takes me for coffee on Thayer Street—exactly what I'm craving, so there's certainly no way I can object to that—and we sit and talk. He's a nice guy. From Wisconsin. First in his family to go to college, even though he swears his father is a genius. He's the oldest of three, with a brother and sister still back in whatever the name of his hometown is.

He tries to forge some kind of connection based on the fact that we're both Midwesterners, but I just don't care. I begin to daydream until he interrupts with questions.

"Huh?"

"How about you? You have any brothers or sisters?"

I look at him. Another blond. His hair is short and wavy, his skin is very white, and his lips are very red. He's not quite funny-looking, but he's not quite handsome either.

"No, I'm an only child," I tell him.

He seems surprised. "Wow, that must be tough," he says, and I can see he regrets having said it almost as soon as he's done speaking.

I get that sometimes: The "poor you, no brothers or sisters to play with" bullshit. But I let it slide. I decide not to tell him that my parents are divorced. Or that I don't get along with my mother.

"I'm really close to my parents," I tell him.

He looks at me, quizzical, and I can tell that the idea of *not* being close to your parents would never even occur to a guy like Tim. And I regret not telling him the truth, rocking his world, or at least giving him an inkling that I'm not whatever he thinks.

I finish my coffee, and I'm feeling better but a bit edgy. Maybe it's all the questions or maybe just the caffeine. Or maybe both. But I'm ready to leave. I look at my watch. It's almost 9:20, and it will take at least ten minutes to get to the observatory.

I need to make another pit stop—that last bit of alcohol filtering through me—but I hate being late and there's no time.

I look up at him. "We need to go."

He hesitates, like he doesn't want it to end, but I get up and he follows. We walk up Thayer, past the northern part of campus, to the observatory on Doyle. He tries to make small talk, mentioning his class schedule and trying to show off a little of his "mastery" of astronomy, but the truth is he's nothing but a lovesick, horny college boy, and I don't have time for it. *Any* of it.

We go into the building about three minutes late, and half the class and the professor—Marsden—are already there. I'm annoyed that we didn't leave earlier.

Professor Marsden is already talking. He's a young guy— hardly older than we are—thin with gold-rimmed glasses and a close-cropped beard, and he clearly loves his subject. He's gesturing and smiling as he tells us about solar flares and sunspots inside the hemisphere dome of the observatory.

The building is old, from the 1880s, brick and brownstone on the outside, but surprisingly modern on the inside. As I look up and around, I can't help but think about the universe, the planets, and all the stars out there. We went to New York once when I was seven, and my dad took me to the Hayden Planetarium. I was so awestruck I didn't want to leave, and we ended up staying until the place closed and they kicked us out. I wonder what my father was like as a young professor, teaching French literature to starry-eyed co-eds back at IU.

Eventually everyone shows, and we take turns looking through the telescope, specially equipped for solar viewing. Our teacher explains the difference between reflectors and refractors and shows us how to adjust the focus, raising his glasses as he looks through the lens.

"It's hit or miss with solar flares," he tells us. "But we've got a good patch of sunspots, and we're right in middle of the 11-year cycle."

When it's my turn, I don't see anything, and I play around with the eyepiece. Then, like a bolt, I see it, the sun, yellow and red, crackling, hot and alive. The corona is crisp and perfectly round, and I can't help but stare at it intently. Then, with no warning, an eruption, like a mountain of flame and gas bursting out and throwing forth.

"Wow!" I exclaim, and there's a chuckle from my class at my enthusiasm.

When I feel the professor's hand on my shoulder, I turn back and realize that he wants to get in for a look. They don't last long, but he manages to see it before it's over.

"Magnificent!" He continues to comment, passing the scope off to Tim, but it's too late. "One of the best ones I've ever seen."

Tim and I are still taking about it walking back down Thayer Street after the class is over. The professor never bothered to take attendance, and I realize that he wasn't being a hard ass when he insisted that we all attend—he just didn't want us to miss out. I used to see that in my dad, when he'd have a class trip to a French movie or a play that he loved. I'm glad I came, glad I saw the sun flaring, free and wild.

Reliving it, I'm free of all the problems in my life, even if just for a moment. As we pass by the Avon, an old-time movie theater that shows classic films, I look up to see what's playing. *Butch Cassidy and the Sundance Kid.* I smile, but only partly because of the ironic name, which is no doubt what Tim thinks when he catches me.

"Want to go?" he asks. "To see the movie I mean."

It was the movie my parents went to see on their first date, when they were both graduate students at Yale. It was the first time they kissed. I think it might have been the first time they did *something else* too. In fact, they used to call *me* the Sundance Kid. Oddly enough, I've never seen the movie myself.

"Yeah, definitely," I tell him, meaning that I *do* want to go but not necessarily with him.

"Great!" he says, unable to hide his shock and glee, and I don't have the energy to correct him. "I'll pick you up at seven."

I say nothing, but I'm ready to burst. *Oh my god, how do I get rid of this guy!* I'll figure it out later. Right now, I need some sleep.

"Do you want some more coffee?" he asks, as we pass the Starbucks.

"No," I say, more firm than he's expecting. "But I do need to use the bathroom."

The coffee has now joined the last bit of booze flushing through me, and I really do need to go.

There's toilet paper this time. Hallelujah! It's when I go to wipe myself that I feel the soreness for the first time. Probing further, it's unmistakable—tenderness—right in my most private parts. Looking back down in the bowl again, there's nothing more from *him*, thank god, but there is a streak, red, there in the water. I look and see it on the toilet tissue too.

I imagine myself being sucked into the sun, burned up, ashes to ashes, and I feel better. *This too shall pass*, my grandfather used to say.

I'm glad in a way. At least I had a good reason for killing him. Then it all comes back at me, and I want to run away, tear my skin off, and die.

I'm quiet for the rest of the walk back.

"Are you okay?" Tim asks.

"Yeah, fine, why?" I say, stopping at the foot of the steps up to my dorm.

"You just looked like—never mind," he says.

I know he wants to walk me all the way to my door, but it's not going to happen. I slip up the stairs, turn my head back, force out a smile, and say 'bye.' And I pull myself inside, closing the outside door after me before he has a chance to follow. I can hear him start to say 'bye' back as the door clicks shut.

If it was a date, I suppose it wasn't a bad one as far as it went. The thing is, I don't really *want* to date. I'm not very social, and I don't like sex that much. Even with Steve it wasn't that great.

Walking up the stairs, I get a weird feeling, like someone's watching me, stalking me. I've been getting it for weeks now, since just after the start of the semester. It comes and goes, but alone there in the stairwell, in the semi-dark, I'm getting it really strong. Hearing my footsteps echo off the concrete, I stop, and the echo stops too.

I'm tempted to head back out, go to where there are more people, maybe get another cup of coffee. But I'm so tired. *No, it's just my imagination. The feeling will go away. It always does.* I pick up the pace and am glad to be back in my room, but the feeling persists. My roommate is gone now, and I pull the drapes closed, undressing in the glow through the curtains. I take everything off except my underwear, and I feel particularly vulnerable until I get my pajamas on and the feeling finally subsides.

I lay in bed thinking about it. *Weird.* Well, given what's happened, maybe not so weird. Then again, this has been happening since way before last night.

Finally, I'm too tired to even think anymore, and I fall off to sleep.

4

I sleepwalk through the next five days, going to my classes, writing an article about a new laboratory on campus for the *Daily Herald,* and completely forgetting about my "second" date with Tim. He doesn't call or leave a message on my phone except the one asking where I was and telling me to call him back. I don't. He hardly acknowledges me in class after that, but I can tell he's furious.

I also scour *The Providence Journal* cover to cover, every day, looking for news of a body in the park. I find the story on page 3 of Tuesday's paper, continued on the front page of the local section. There's a recent picture of him, and I worry that someone who was at the dean's party will recognize him and connect him to me, but most students, and faculty for that matter, don't read the local paper.

I'm pretty sure that no one saw us together, but I decide to cut my hair anyway. I'll have it done at the place on Wickenden Street after my last class on Friday, before I get on the plane. That way, everyone'll think it was just something I had done over break. I also decide to keep wearing my glasses. I can't afford new lenses anyway, and the combination of that with the new hairstyle should stop anyone from recognizing me from that night.

Finally, it's Friday afternoon, and I'm almost out of here. I've been a wreck for the past 24 hours, convinced the police were going to knock on my door, but it doesn't look like they have a clue. I know it doesn't really make any sense, but I feel like if I can just make it out of here, get on that plane for Indiana, I'm home free. I leave for the airport in two hours. Getting back to my room, I call for a cab at four and grab my dirty laundry.

I hate going home with a suitcase full of dirty clothes, so I always do my laundry before I go. I take off my pants, socks, and top and throw them in the pile, putting on my laundry uniform—a ratty pink skirt with a stretched hem that's just a little too short, a pair of black canvas sneakers, and an old, white Banana Republic t-shirt with a vest pocket that's torn at the corner.

The dorm is practically empty—half the kids took off early for Ft. Lauderdale or some other horrible place and the other half are home or on their way there. I see one other girl in the laundry room, we smile at each other, say hello, and I dump my clothes in, heading off to get my haircut.

I was kind of bummed about it at first—that is, about having to get my hair cut, but I eventually decided that it's a good thing. I've been wearing my Prince Valiant cut since I was fifteen, and it's starting to look a little square, even for me. I looked through a few magazines and decided on a French bob. I'm still a little nervous about it, but the woman at the beauty salon tells me it'll look great, and *she* looks great, so I sit back and let it happen.

When she hands me the mirror, I put on my glasses, and *wow!*—it *does* look great. I wish I had enough money for a bigger tip, but she seems happy with what I give her. Back at the dorm, I finish my laundry, pack, and get my cab with fifteen minutes to spare.

Security at the airport—even a little one like T. F. Green—always makes me nervous, and I worry a little that I no longer look like the picture on my Indiana driver's license, but the man behind the counter hardly looks at me. Ditto for the guy at the scanner, and, even though I should be glad, it kind of bums me out that no one is noticing my new haircut.

I make it through the scanner without a hitch but then get pulled out of line for a random search. It's a woman this time, and she gives me the third degree, which makes me think how ridiculous the whole process is. Here I am, I probably killed someone less than a week ago, and they're searching me for hair gel!

The woman feels up and down my legs, up under my skirt, and then under my arms and over my chest. She's short, fat, and ugly, and I feel like killing *her.*

She looks at my license for what seems like an incredibly long time, and then up at my face, and I begin to get nervous.

"Emily Catherine Williams?" she asks, meeting my eyes.

"Yeah," I say, trying to figure her dour expression. "I just got my hair cut."

But she doesn't care. "Where are you heading?"

"Bloomington, Indiana," I tell her. *It's the Paris of southwest Indiana*, I think, fighting a smile.

"You can go," she tells me, finally.

I can still feel her rubber-gloved hands on my thighs as I walk away. My nerves don't calm until the plane takes off an hour later.

The guy next to me is sucking down a Bloody Mary, and watching him mix the two little bottles of vodka into his tomato juice, I fight the urge to have a drink myself. I don't have the money for it anyway.

He notices me looking over and starts talking to me. He's middle-aged and just being friendly, but I don't really feel like talking. He tells me he's got a son in college who didn't get into Brown, and I feel bad.

I have to change planes in Newark and again in Chicago, and it's almost ten o'clock before we land. I got seated next to a fat woman who smelled on the second leg but got the whole row to myself on the last leg to Indianapolis.

I'm curled up asleep, having a nightmare about Danny, dead, in the park, when the stewardess wakes me for landing. Pulling off the blanket, I'm cold and reach into my bag and put on an oversized sweatshirt.

When we land and I finally escape the plane, I can't wait to get home. I'm still wearing my laundry suit plus the giant sweatshirt, and I'm sure I look awful. I stop in the ladies' room to use the bathroom and survey the damage. I *do* look awful, shapeless under my wrinkled clothes. Even my new haircut is messed up.

I comb it out as best as I can and debate changing my clothes, but I don't even have my suitcase yet. Besides, it's just my dad.

When I finally get out of the terminal, he's there waiting. He sees me, gets out of the car, and hugs me.

"Hey sweetie," he says, and I burst into tears.

He pulls back to look at me. "What's wrong, Emmie?"

He looks so worried. It makes me glad that someone cares so much but terrible at the same time. If he only knew.

"Nothing. It was just such a long trip, and I'm getting my period."

He rubs my back before throwing my suitcase in the trunk, making an embarrassed grimace, but saying nothing more. It works every time.

Then, in a weird twist, a minute or two later, sitting there in the car on the ride back to Bloomington, I *do* get my period. I'd actually been worried about it. It wasn't the right time of the month, but I knew Danny didn't use protection. And, as they say, you can get pregnant anytime. I mean I wasn't too worried—I could feel it coming—but still, it's a relief to actually have it happen.

My dad looks over at me. "You look different."

I smile at him, and he knows he's going to have to figure it out on his own. A second later, flipping his eyes between me and the road, the light bulb goes on.

"You're wearing your glasses!"

I roll my eyes. My dad likes me in glasses.

He looks a little confused. He's a smart man, very smart, in fact, but he's a little absent-minded. He and my mother were kind of an odd couple. She's tall and blond, from Boston, English ancestry back to the Mayflower, smart, unbelievably beautiful, and a huge snob.

He's a native Midwesterner, from Chicago, with French Canadian and Dutch ancestors. He's average height and build, but always disheveled, unpretentious, and kind to a fault. I know he wanted more children, but mother couldn't

stand what it did to her body. I'm pretty sure I was an acci-
dent, but I know how much my father loves me.

My parents actually got married when they were still in
graduate school, and they both got tenure track positions in
the French department at IU. My mother published lots of
papers, wrote three books, and got tenure when I was about
ten, but my father didn't. He was too focused on teaching,
cared too much about his students, and they hung him out
to dry.

After that, it was only a matter of time. My grandfather
never liked his son-in-law, and my father's career downturn
just made it worse. He couldn't even get a job teaching at my
prep school and ended up at a ghetto public school, fleshing
out his income with tutoring. He was planning on writing a
novel in French about a Canadian Mountie in love with a
French Canadian beauty in 1850s Quebec, but it never quite
happened.

Meanwhile, my mother divorced him, met someone
else, and got remarried. She moved over to the campus in
Indianapolis, where he had tenure, and she's been there ever
since. *Uncle Billy*, she told me to call him. Yeah, right. She
ended up divorcing him too.

My father continues to look me over, still trying to figure
it out. "Is that a new dress?" he asks, and I slump in my seat.

Unable to stand it any more, I blurt it out. "I got my hair
cut!" I tell him, smiling.

"Oh yeah, it looks great." He says, finally realizing.

My dad is really cute. I wish he would find somebody,
but there's no chance. I wonder if my haircut really looks any
good.

The trip to Bloomington is over an hour, especially the way my dad drives. He's still got the same Honda Civic he had when I was in high school, even more rust popping through the oxidized white paint, and he drives like an old man.

I put my feet up on the dashboard and put the seat back and relax. I can see my underwear in the reflection inside the windshield, and I think about men and dating and my mind wanders.

Is my butt really that big? No wonder Steve broke up with me. Maybe it's just the curvature of the windshield. I stare at it. No, god, I do have a fat ass. I have a fat ass, and that's why Steve broke up with me.

Steve . . .

I wonder if he's home or if he went off to Florida or somewhere else. I saw him a couple of days ago on campus, but he didn't even say hello. Steve . . . I sigh, but my dad doesn't notice, or maybe he just thinks I'm tired, which I am.

Steve . . . Steven J. Smith. Can you get any more vanilla than that? I met him on my first day of kindergarten, and we walked to school together every day until 8th grade, when I went off to Prep. But I'd still see him two or three times a week and at least once on the weekends. He only lived two blocks down, and his mother used to joke that some day we'd get married.

But really, he was more of a best friend—at least the closest thing to a best friend that *I* ever had. He went to Bloomington South, the local public high school, and he seemed to like it pretty well, but I think he was a little jealous that I was at Prep, but just a little. By ninth grade, we would talk on the phone every night, at least on the days when we didn't see each other, and we started to go to football games together.

Nothing ever happened—we really were just friends—until October of my senior year. It was the Halloween party at Rutherford, a Saturday night soirée. I was dressed like a 1920s flapper, and he like Jay Gatsby. We ended up sitting spraddle-legged on the tennis court, hip-to-hip, drinking beer out of large plastic cups. It took a lot to get me drunk, even then, but I had a pretty good buzz on. I looked over at him, my best friend, dressed like the Great Gatsby. He was so handsome! And just like that, I wanted him to kiss me, but he didn't.

Later that year, in the spring, he took me to my senior prom. *I* actually asked *him*, but we both understood that we were just going as friends. A couple of other guys had actually already asked me, and they were hardly geeks, but I barely knew them, so I said no. I was surprised but not interested, but I did want to go.

So I went with Steve, and we had a blast. Afterwards, he took me home, and I went up to my room alone and got drunk, and the matter of whether or not he'd ever kiss me seemed settled. Then we spent all summer together. I was headed off to Brown in the fall, and he was staying in Bloomington, headed to IU.

He was a lifeguard at the lake near where we lived, and I went and hung out everyday, through long, hot summer days.

I wasn't drinking much then; I was happy, hanging out on the fake sand beach in my orange bikini, joking with Steve, and getting a Midwestern tan under a pair of oak trees. And, for the first time, I started to really fall in love.

As summer waned, a certain sadness began to well up in me. I'd never been happier in my life, carefree, college acceptance in hand, hanging out with my best friend, who increasingly felt like my boyfriend. But it was all about to end. I was heading off to Providence, and he was staying there in Bloomington. There was always the phone, but long distance never works. So this would be the end.

I wanted desperately to give him something, something of me, and I knew what that had to be. I hadn't wanted to go off to college a virgin—I'd been thinking about that for a while—and now I could kill two birds with one stone.

I was so nervous, I put it off for almost two weeks, until it was the last day of summer before they closed the lake for swimming.

"I want to show you something in the guard shack," I said, taking his hand and smiling, leading the way.

Touching his hand felt electric. He must have felt it too, but I don't think he knew what to make of it.

"What?" he asked, smiling back, a little tense, anticipating.

"I have something for you," I said, opening the door, pulling him inside, and closing it behind us.

There was no lock, but no one would be coming in. I didn't have a plan, but nervous energy, my passion, and my hormones took over, and I touched his face, and we started kissing.

It was awkward but delicious, and we tangled over to a bench a few feet away in the tiny room, and I sat down on top of him, my hip turned into his lap. We were both in bathing suits—me in my orange bikini, and him in his blue surfer boxers—and we kept kissing, not really knowing what to do next. He was a virgin too, but I could feel that he wanted me, and it was surprising and wonderful.

We kissed for a long while, until I ended up sitting directly in his lap, facing away from him, and it happened. It was awkward, and it hurt, and it was over too fast. I didn't even get my bathing suit off. But I was glad that it happened, glad to be so close, so connected. The second I was able, I turned around and told him that I loved him. He bristled, afraid, and my heart sank. But I was still glad we did it. I only saw him once after that before I went away to school.

We didn't talk for almost a year. No phone calls, no get-togethers when I was home for winter break, nothing. Then, finally, in the spring, I wrote him a long letter. He didn't answer, and I didn't know why. I thought maybe it was some sort of cosmic punishment for what I did to Willie. But that's just crazy.

Then, back at Brown, the first week of my sophomore year, I ran into him on campus. He had transferred. He was afraid to talk to me, said he never got the letter.

But he seemed really glad to see me. We had a long talk and wound up back in my dorm room. It was much better this time. And I knew enough to keep my mouth shut. But that was it. I hardly saw him after that. He seemed to find his place at the school, his crowd, and I wasn't in it. But whenever I'd see him on campus, if I was with a guy, even though there was never anything going on, he'd give me this jealous glare. And then there were the phone calls.

Creepy, silent calls, always from a private number. Breathing, hard through flared nostrils, for five or ten seconds until one of us hung up. I had no idea who it was, but the calls followed me home on vacations, and that made me think of Steve.

We're at the house now. I'm so tired, I can barely move, but it's good to be home. Following my father through the front door, I climb the half-staircase to the upper hallway, and find my room. It's a plain house, split-level, three bedroom, two and a half bath, but I like it.

"You look very pretty," I hear my father call out.

"Huh?" I answer, barely able to keep my eyes open.

"Your haircut," he says. "It's very nice."

I smile. "Thanks Dad."

The interaction wakes me up just enough to get into my pajamas, brush my teeth, and get into bed. A minute later, I'm asleep.

5

The next morning, I wake up from another bad dream: I dreamt I was having sex with my father. Oh my god, what is wrong with me! Professor Mankow would have a field day. I was a psych major at one point, and I feel like I belong in a textbook. *The case of Miss Emily Williams. Murderer. Reverse Oedipal Complex. Wanted to kill her mother and marry her father. Tore out her contact lenses and had to wear glasses.* It sounds like something from *The Brown Film Bulletin,* and I giggle to myself.

I reach for my glasses, but I can't find them. Then I realize that I fell asleep with them on. It's happened to me before. I'm not used to them, so I forgot. Now there'll be marks on my face. I get up and look at myself in the mirror. Yeah, red marks on the bridge of my nose. I actually have a nice nose, straight and just the right size. It fits my face. I brush my teeth again and catch my eye in the mirror and the dream comes back. My dad! Ugh!

Don't get me wrong, my dad is a good guy. I mean I wouldn't mind marrying him. I mean someone *like* him. Well, maybe someone who notices me a little more. He always noticed my mom. Of course she's a lot prettier than I am. And I really don't hate her. I just wish I *liked* her more. Looking at my eyes, I wonder what it would be like to look like her.

It's a little after nine, and I'm supposed to go up to school, Rutherford Prep that is, my old haunt, to meet Mr. Hanson, my old English teacher. I'd sent him an email from Providence, telling him about my predicament—my *academic* predicament—and asking if he had any suggestions. He told me to come up to his office, and we'd talk about it. Said he'd be there Saturday morning doing grades for second trimester.

I said I'd be there at ten, and I'm regretting it now. I'm tired and I've got cramps. Maybe I should have waited a couple of days. No, it's better to get it out of the way. Besides, he was my favorite teacher, and I'm looking forward to seeing him. We used to talk for hours up in his office. He wrote his undergraduate thesis on Fitzgerald, who happens to be my favorite. So we hit it off right away.

I sit on the toilet grimacing through cramps and texting him to confirm, when my father yells upstairs that breakfast is ready. I can tell from his voice that he's made something special for me, probably chocolate chip pancakes, my favorite, but I feel like screaming.

"I'll be right down!" I yell.

I finish my text and think about taking a shower but decide to do it after breakfast. Putting myself back together, the pain subsides a little, and I head downstairs and enter the kitchen.

Yup, chocolate chip pancakes. Getting a whiff, I realize how hungry I am. My dad is already eating. He's just an okay cook, but this is the one thing he really makes well, and I savor every bite, washing it down with a big glass of whole milk.

He asks what I have planned for the day, and I tell him I'm going over to see Mr. Hanson, but he doesn't seem to be listening. There's something else on his mind.

"Emily," he starts. No more *Emmie . . . Emily,* and I know it's going to be bad. "We need to talk about school."

We need to talk. From my dad! I start to mumble something about how I went to see the dean, and I'm working on a new schedule, but he cuts me off.

"I don't have the money to pay for you to be a student up there anymore." His words shock me, but they shouldn't. "You know the deal. Your mother paid half, and I paid half."

"I had a scholarship," I say in protest. And it's true. I had a merit scholarship and even a few bucks from the Latin prize. But it only paid about half the bill, even with a fifty percent discount for being a professor's kid.

It's also true that financial aid covered about half the rest, but that still left $6,000 a year that my parents had to pay. They agreed to split it down the middle, even though my mother made it clear that she was doing more, since her employer (she still had the professorship) was responsible for the discount.

"I know, sweetheart," he says. I can see that he's pained. "But you were also supposed to finish in four years."

His words sting me. I'm not used to my father being tough. I know he's right, but I feel hurt and betrayed. I had a scholarship. And financial aid. My parents were supposed to pay for the rest.

"Four years, kiddo, that's it."

I feel like he's kicking me in the stomach, but I get it. Four years. And I'm in my fifth. Already on borrowed time, and graduation still nowhere in sight.

Looking at him, I can see: My dad really is tapped out. It was my grandfather's money which even paid his part. I think to rub his nose in it, but I can't do it. I'm mad at him, but deep down, I know it's my own fault. So there it is: You had five years to get your diploma on someone else's dime, Emily Catherine. After that, you're on your own. So, I'm on my own.

With nothing left to say, I get up and leave. I don't even look at him. I'm feeling weak and nauseous, and I barely make it back up to my bed.

Closing the door behind me, I curl up on the covers. The cramps are killing me. It hurts so much now I can't even straighten out. It's 9:41, and I'm supposed to be at school in 19 minutes.

Reaching over, I grab for my phone on the nightstand but can't reach it. It's almost too much to move at this point, but I lift myself up until I have it in my hand then plop back down into my curled-up position.

Texting Mr. Hanson, I let him know that I'm running late. He always seems to tap right into these things and tells me not to worry: he'll be there until noon. Even his text messages are written in full, clear, grammatically correct sentences.

Laying there on the bed, I relax a little. That sugar-bomb breakfast is starting to give me a little more energy, and I roll over and get up. For a few seconds, my whole body seems ready to cramp up, and I almost get back into bed, but it eases off a bit, and I stumble into the bathroom.

Opening the medicine cabinet, I find the Costco-sized bottle of Advil, open it, and swallow four, leaning over to wash them down with a handful of Bloomington tap. I turn the shower on, and a minute later I'm under a hot stream. The hot water feels good, and I linger in the shower for a while, washing my hair and letting the Advil kick in.

When I'm done, I feel almost normal, at least compared to before. I take the time to unpack my suitcase, taking out clothes for the day.

I put on a white top and socks, but I can't get my jeans on over my big fat hips. I know I'm bloated, but that's only part of it. Even without getting on the scale, I know I'm probably pushing 130. I shouldn't have had those pancakes. Then the cramps hit me all over again.

I lay back for a minute and they go away. Finally, still laying there on the bed, I manage to squeeze my jeans over my butt. Serves me right for putting them in the dryer. But I was in a hurry. Plane to catch and all.

Checking the weather, I decide to put on a sweater. The yellow one, monogrammed under the neck, that my mother gave me last Christmas. Grabbing the hair dryer, I brush my hair out. I have straight hair, easy to manage, and the bob falls right back into place.

It's almost 11 o'clock, and I'm finally ready. I check myself out in the mirror, front, back, and side. A little bloated, even under the sweater. And a little too much on the hips and backside, but I like my hair, and there's nothing I can do about the rest right now anyway.

On a whim, I take out the tape measure and brace for the worst: Bust, still 33″, waist, used to be 27, now 28. Hips, 38¾. 38¾! They used to be 37. *Fat and about to leave college without a degree.* I exit the house without saying goodbye to my dad.

On my way over, I replay the whole thing in my head. I know it's not his fault, but I can't help it, I'm still mad at my dad. Then I think about what I'm going to say to Mr. Hanson. I was his favorite student, at least I think I was, and I know he had high hopes for me. I'm sure he'll be disappointed. Then again, he already knows I have my flaws.

I'm pretty sure he knows I drink. And I'm pretty sure he's something of a drinker—a social drinker at least—himself. I also know he's gay, so it would be safe for us to be drinking buddies I guess, but I don't want to. It's different for him. Vintage wines and expensive Sherries. A nice buzz. A lot classier and more in control than my Comfort-soaked forays in parks and storage rooms with rough men who want to plant their flag in me, so to speak.

No, Mr. Hanson is a cocktail party type, our very own Noel Coward, loosening up over a glass of hundred year old port and telling an amusing story about the time he met Truman Capote at a party in the Village when he was a student in New York.

I know he was married at one point. And I think he might have even loved her. But it didn't work out. I'm sure he didn't love her in the way she wanted.

I'm still thinking about it when I approach the school. Circling the grounds, I pray I don't see the caretaker or anyone else. But I do hear the sound of a mower, coming from around the other side, I think, then silence, as I finally get to the front entrance.

It feels a little weird to walk into the building, especially empty. The lights aren't even on, but there's enough daylight coming in to light the hallways in a dull cast. The windows, paned glass, make patterns on the floor, falling in and out of line with the light and dark linoleum tiles.

The school itself dates from the 1880s, but this building (and the new campus) went up in the fifties—institutional and proper but not much charm. It was a boys' school originally, until the mid-70s, but the converted bathrooms and class pictures up on the walls are the only clues these days.

Heading up the stairs, I look at my cell phone. 11:23. Not bad.

I'm feeling better too. The Advil, the hot shower, and stretching my legs seem to have done the trick.

The second floor is darker, and I get that odd feeling again, like I'm being watched, but I see the open door at the end of the hall, lights on, and the feeling is gone. A head pops out the doorway. Mr. Hanson.

6

He looks exactly the same as the last time I saw him a year and a half ago. He's got the same wrinkles around his mouth. When he sees me, he smiles and the wrinkles deepen. He's got a warm friendly face—a slightly ruddy complexion under a shock of medium dark hair, graying a little. And round horn-rimmed glasses that fit his face perfectly, magnifying clear blue eyes. He always wears a sport coat, a nice pair of slacks, and a button down shirt. And always but always a bow tie.

"Hi Mr. Hanson," I say, like I'm still in high school English.

He waves me in with almost theatrical animation. "Emily! Come in, have a seat."

Sitting across from him behind his big metal desk, I remember all the hours we talked in this office about books and authors and where to go to college.

He clasps his hands behind his head and leans back. "So what's the trouble?"

I like the way he cuts right to the chase, still easygoing, like whatever it is can be fixed, like there's no doubt that everything will be fine.

"My father is cutting me loose," I tell him.

He furls his eyebrows. "Bob? I don't believe it."

"Well, maybe not exactly cutting me loose," I say, called out. Then I tell him the story—just the part about school and how I started as a psych major then switched to biology then modern culture and media, and now I'm not sure what I want, and I'm going into the last leg of my fifth year, an unfocused mess, and my father is pulling the plug.

"What about Celia?"

Yes, my mother. He always refers to my parents by their first names. The truth is, my mother might actually be willing to throw in a few more bucks but only to avoid the shame, or, if you want to look at it another way, to have the glory of that Ivy League degree bestowed on *her* child. But it doesn't matter, because I'd never ask her. I'd rather wait tables.

I shake my head, and Mr. H seems to get it without further explanation. He's met her enough times and heard me talk about her.

"How are your grades?"

Finally something to smile about. "A couple of B's, the rest A's. I had a 3.8 something the last time I checked."

He gives a proud little smile and nods, raising his eyebrows just enough to say *you're a smart one*, and I feel good for the first time all day.

"Well," he says. "Let's sit down and figure out how close you are to graduation in each of those majors."

I shrug and shake my head. "But I'm not even sure what I want to do with my life or what concentration I even want."

Looking at me then down at his desk, he frowns and shakes his head. "It doesn't matter. The goal is to graduate, get your degree. You've got terrific grades, a great transcript. With that Brown degree in hand, you'll be able to do whatever you want." He looks straight at me. "I know a guy who majored in English and became a banker and another one who studied engineering and went into the movie business. The point is to focus and get your degree."

Maybe he's right. But still, it seems like I have such a long way to go and no money. "What about the money?"

He makes an uncertain gesture but tightens his gaze. "If you have a plan and a timetable, I'm sure Bob will help out. I also think you should get a job."

I figured this was coming, but I'm okay with it. If I'm paying for part of it, my dad will be more inclined to meet me halfway. After all, he wants me to graduate. I nod. "One of the diners in downtown Providence is always looking for waitresses."

Mr. H pulls out a piece of paper, and waves me over to sit next to him behind his desk. We spend the next fifteen or twenty minutes figuring out how close I am to a degree in each of the three fields. It turns out that I need only six more classes to get my degree in biology. But that would still be a year.

Then I remember the article I wrote about the new lab. "Maybe I can get a lab job and add it to my schedule as a research course and kill two birds with one stone. If I do that for the summer and fall and take two other regular courses in each term, I'll be done by December. And I'll be earning some money at the same time."

I still need to convince my dad, and I'll probably still need to take out a student loan, but I'm feeling good about it.

Mr. Hanson smiles at me. "Sounds like you've got a plan."

"Thanks, Mr. H," I say with a wistful, grateful smile.

He looks at me with affection but a little discomfit. "One more thing, Emily." He pauses and looks straight at me, still sitting there next to him. "Stop drinking."

"I *don't* drink," I tell him, defensive.

He puts his hand up, as if to tell me to save it for someone else. "You're a good person, smart, pretty, responsible." He sighs and girds himself. "Bob is really a lucky guy. If I ever had a daughter, I'd want her to be just like you. Except for *that*. But, you know, no one's perfect. Get help if you need it, but stop."

There's a moment of silence, and I look right into his eyes, fearful. "Don't tell my dad."

The calm reassurance returns to his face, and I see those wrinkles deepen again. "No, Emily, never."

If he weren't such a crusty old WASP, he'd probably hug me now, and we'd both feel uncomfortable, but the moment ends there.

We talk for a while longer, and I remember how much I like Mr. Hanson. I wonder now how many more times I'll ever see him in my life. I have a lump in my throat when I say goodbye.

It's after three when I leave, and my high from the meeting wears off quickly. Is the plan really all that solid? I still need to get into that lab. The Advil is wearing off too, and my dad's words are still ringing in my ears. And now my old teacher's too.

When I get back to the house, I'm ready to curl back up on my bed.

"How is Mr. Hanson, honey?" my dad asks.

"Okay," I say, not feeling inclined to elaborate.

I need to think about it some more; I need to rest; and I'm still pissed off.

I go up to my room and curl up on my bed still in my clothes. When I wake up, it's almost 5:30, and I feel gross. I'm starving, but all I can think about is sugar. At least I don't feel like a drink.

The pain is back, but I don't really like taking too much Advil—my mother's friend went into kidney failure from it—so I decide to just rough it.

Thinking about how Mr. Hanson said I was a good person, I suddenly remember the boy I killed and Willie with the awl in his chest. *No, I'm not*, I think to myself. But maybe it's not too late, not too late to change. I can at least try.

I pull off my clothes, finally free of those jeans, stripping down to my panties. Even my pajamas don't feel good, and I opt for nothing more than the oversized sweatshirt. I'm swimming in it, and I'm sure I look ridiculous, but it just about covers my underwear, and it's actually comfortable.

I make my way down to the TV room, adjacent to the kitchen, grabbing a box of Captain Crunch, a half gallon carton of milk, and a bowl and a spoon on the way in. My dad is sitting there reading *The New York Times*.

"Mind if I watch TV?" I ask.

He knows I get like this when I'm having my period, so he's less inclined to argue. The truth is, though, the man could read in the middle of a wind tunnel and not be distracted, so he's probably just being honest if he says no.

I'm surprised when he gets up and leaves. I turn on the TV and start watching *Tom and Jerry*, but I'm still thinking about Mr. Hanson. How did he know? What else does he know? I'm sure he doesn't know anything else. But is it that obvious? No, he's just really tuned in. Nothing to worry about.

I dig into the cereal: Captain Crunch, the perfect combination of sweet and salty. Just what I'm craving. I sit for the better part of the next two days, finishing two boxes and a half gallon of milk, watching cartoons and reruns. *I Dream of Jeannie*, *The Bob Newhart Show*, *I Love Lucy*, and *That Girl*. I wish I were Marlo Thomas in New York, with a huge apartment and a handsome fiancé. Well, maybe I don't. No, I think I do.

My dad is in and out. The phone rings occasionally, and, after a few rings, if he doesn't pick up, I go to answer it. The vague thought that it could be my stalker crosses my mind, but it's just students looking for tutoring or telemarketers. Finally, the last call is my mother, and I sort of wish I hadn't answered it.

"Hello, sweetie," she says.

"Hi Mom."

The conversation seems to end right there. We basically never have anything to say to each other, but she can't just let it go. I guess I don't blame her.

"Are you home for break?"

"Yeah, until Sunday."

"Oh good. Are you having fun with your father?"

"Yeah."

"Good, good. Is he there?"

"No, he didn't pick up, so I guess he must be out." There's a pause. It must have sounded odd the way I said it. "I was taking a nap, downstairs in the TV room," I add as a sort of explanation.

"Oh, okay," she says. "I won't disturb you then. Just tell your father I called."

No it's okay Mom, if you want to talk, talk to me, I'd like that, I want to say, but I don't.

"Okay, Mom. Bye."

A minute later, I'm back on the couch eating the last bits of cereal, having run out of milk about an hour ago. *Jeannie* is on, and I look at the TV behind my toenails. The nail polish is chipping, and I need to re-do them. It's the only girly-girl thing I really do, a habit I picked up from a girl named Jenny on the field hockey team.

They're a kind of metallic purple, and I go upstairs during a commercial to find more. I have five or six colors in the medicine cabinet but finally narrow it down to two. I can't decide. Looking at the names, I see the lighter shade is called "I'm Not Really a Waitress." So-so. I look at the darker one. When I see that that one is named "I Dream of Jeannie," the deal is sealed.

By the time I'm done, I'm halfway through *Batman* and ready for more cereal. It's a little after one on Monday afternoon, and my dad is back, so I can take the car. I don't really feel like going out, but I want more cereal. It's funny, but I'm not craving a drink at all.

Going back upstairs, I do another little jiggle on my bed to get my jeans back on. It's a little easier this time—

loosened by my outing to Rutherford—but I haven't been dressed for two days, so it's a wash as far as comfort goes. I find my father in his bedroom, reading some book on Molière, and I ask if I can borrow the car. "Sure, just be careful with it," he says joking, and I smile at him for the first time since our fight.

I tell him about the phone calls, including the one from my mother, and he takes it in. He tells me he wants to go out to dinner later, and even though I can't even think about it, I smile again and say okay. He wants to go to the French place downtown, *Chez Jardin*, which we both like, and I appreciate the gesture. It won't happen for several more hours, so I'll have time to get myself ready.

Taking the keys, I slip into my black canvas sneakers and head out. It feels funny to drive at first—I think the last time I was behind the wheel was last summer—but I get used to it again fast. A few minutes later, I'm pulling in at the 7-Eleven. I hope they have Captain Crunch.

It takes me a minute, but I'm relieved to find it. Grabbing a gallon of milk, I go to check out. And there, standing behind some guy with two sixes, I hear the bell ring—someone coming through the door—and turn to see Steve entering the store.

Heading straight back for the freezer case, he doesn't seem to see me, and I don't want him to. I haven't taken a shower in two days, and I look awful. I'm still wearing the same oversized sweatshirt, my smallish boobs disappearing under the waves of fabric. I'm not even wearing socks. Or a bra. Even my new haircut is a mess. I'm sure I stink.

Not turning around, I wait for the checkout guy to take the guy's money in front of me. It seems to take forever, but it's finally my turn.

"Ten seventy-six," he tells me.

I'm shocked that it's so expensive, but what did I expect at a convenience store? I snap my wallet open, pull out a ten and fumble for change, actually finding three quarters and a penny. I take the bag and leave, seeing Steve turn towards me just as I exit. I'm not really sure if he sees me or not. I don't think so. But he might not have said anything anyway. Why is he such a dick to me?

I dump the bag on the passenger seat, and pull out without looking through the windshield and back into the store. I'm home in five minutes and back in my underwear, fresh bowl of double C in hand in ten.

I admire my toenails. I have cute feet. Cute feet and a nice nose. The rest of me is so-so, but right now, I don't care.

A few hours later, and it's time to get ready for dinner. It feels good to take a shower. I still don't feel great, but it's tolerable. I decide to dress up a little, picking out a nice pair of black pants with a matching jacket—I'm feeling a little bad about my dad and decide to bury the hatchet. I mean he paid for the ticket to fly me out here, and I've hardly talked to him since Saturday. Besides, I want to tell him about my plan. I really want him on board. In fact, I *need* him on board.

My outfit is a little tight around the waist but comfortable everywhere else. I check myself out in the mirror. Not *too* bad, I think.

The restaurant is downtown, on the other side of the university, about a twenty minute drive. We're about halfway there when I start to talk.

"I'm sorry Daddy," I say, turning to him. I'm already crying. God, I didn't mean to, but I can't help it.

He turns to me, a little surprised, but he warms up fast. "It's okay, baby."

"I know you're disappointed, I know it's all my fault, I know how expensive it is . . ." I start to really blubber.

I half expect him to tell me it'll be alright, but he doesn't. I know my dad is tapped, and it makes me feel rotten.

"I'm going to get a job. I want to finish. I want you to be proud of me."

"I *am* proud of you," he says.

When we get to *Chez Jardin*, he gives the attendant the key—yes, it's one of those places—and I stand, arms around myself, cheeks still wet, feeling embarrassed. I forgot to bring tissue, and I wipe my tears on my sleeve, but it's synthetic and doesn't hold the moisture.

By the time we get our table, I'm okay, and I tell my dad my plan. I tell him that I'll get a second job as a waitress or something if I have to. He puts his arm around me in the booth and pulls me in to him in a long-awaited gesture of pride, and I'm ready to start crying all over again. It feels funny being in such a big booth, just the two of us, and, inexplicably, I wish my mother were here too. And maybe a little brother or a sister.

The food comes. It's really first rate here. People don't believe it, right here in the middle of Indiana, but my dad knows the owner, a fellow graduate student who also gave up on academia, and he really knows his stuff.

I finish my steak au poivre, and I'm just digging in to my crème brûlée, when my dad tells me he'll help through the end of the year.

"Thank you Daddy," I tell him. This is really what I needed to make it all work, and I finish my dessert, happy for now.

When we get home, the phone is ringing, and I answer it. I have a feeling it's my mother again. Strangely, I actually want it to be my mother, but it isn't. The flared breathing, angry and heavy comes through the earpiece instead, telling me it's someone else. I wait five, ten seconds and then hang up, sick to my stomach.

"Who was it, sweetie?" my dad asks, following me in.

"Wrong number," I tell him.

"Want to watch a movie?" he asks, unaware.

"No, I'm tired," I say.

Four hours later, I'm still staring up at the ceiling in the dark, lying in my bed.

7

By Wednesday afternoon, I feel almost normal again. The bloating is just about gone and so are the cramps. And I haven't gotten any more phone calls, but I'm not answering the phone anymore either.

I put on sweats and go out for a jog. I'm not a big exercise hound, but it feels like I've been cooped up forever, and I need to get out and blow off a little steam.

Running down towards the university, I replay all the conversations in my mind. Things are back to normal with my dad, and I'm glad for that. I have a plan going forward for school, and I don't want to get my hopes up, but I think it might actually work. The phone calls, well, they've been going on for a while, so I'm not going to worry about them.

And I'm not going to worry about Steve either. If he wants to talk, he knows where to find me. And if he can't get his act together, maybe I'm better off without him. It's a hard thing for me to say. I mean, I've known him forever, and he was my first. And my second. And my only. I feel a pang and have to stop for a minute. A drink, that's what I need. I know what my mother would say. You'll find some-body else. The thought helps. The urge is still there—both for him and the drink—but not as much. I know it'll be back, but I've kept it at bay, at least for now, and start run-ning again.

I pass the soccer stadium on the north side of campus, and I make a loop around it, heading back in the other direc-tion for home.

Inevitably, Danny and that night in the park creeps into my head, but I've got that under control too. He raped me, and I killed him. He deserved it, I tell myself, and I pick up my stride.

By the time I'm back home, I'm soaked with sweat, but I feel good. A few months of this and I'll be slim as a rail.

By Thursday afternoon, I'm starting to get bored. It happens when I'm home for a while. I actually re-read *Gatsby* and start on *Benjamin Button* but get sick of it halfway through. I'm in the living room, still wearing the same jeans (different shirt) and feel like putting my pajamas back on, but they really need to be washed. So do the jeans. I decide to do a load of laundry. I'll probably do another one on Sunday before I go back and could get away with waiting, but it'll give me something to do for a little while.

I go up to my bedroom, take off my clothes, put on my laundry suit, and make a pile. There's hardly enough to fill half a load, but I'm glad I'm doing it. I'm running low on underwear anyway, and I want clean jammies.

I go down two half-levels to the rec room and pile the laundry against the top loader. Setting it going, I'm left with a half hour to kill and nothing to do. Back to square one. I look around. Except for the basement under the entry level, this is the bottom level of the house, right under the bedrooms.

I used to play here when I was a kid, and some of my toys are still here, in large drawers under the bench opposite the bar. *The bar.* I don't dare even take a peek. It's piled up with junk anyway. My parents never used it, and I turn my focus back to the rest of the room. My field hockey stuff is down here somewhere too. Scanning the linoleum tiled floor, white and green, I take the room in. It used to be my favorite room in the house, even more than my bedroom, even after I fell and broke my arm down here when I was twelve, but I can't for the life of me remember why.

My dad's computer is over in the corner. I'd forgotten that he'd set up a sort of makeshift office down here. He did most of his tutoring at his students' houses and up in the living room when they came here, but he liked to have a place to go to do his own work, away from everything else. And I suddenly remember why I like it down here so much.

I go over to turn the computer on and check my email. It takes a minute to boot, and it occurs to me that something or other might not actually be working—my dad's not the most tech-savvy guy in the world—but a minute later, I'm on.

Nothing but junk mail. Then a note from my astronomy professor to the class—just a syllabus addendum, boring stuff. More junk: A penis enlargement ad addressed to Mr. Evan Williams—don't know how they got that one; a scam email from Nigeria; and another one from Romania. Then I notice an email from Tim. *Tim.* Ugh. I cringe thinking of the fake date that he tricked me into that morning and delete it without reading it. My eye catches the subject on the way to the trash bin: *I need to talk to you.* "I don't think so," I say to myself.

I put my clothes in the dryer, hang up my jeans, and go back to surfing the web. I look up the *ProJo* on a whim just to see if there's anything about Danny. Not expecting there to be anything more, I'm surprised to see an article with links to a video clip from the local Providence news. I watch it, volume low, like a guilty child. I guess I am.

His name was Danny Marcone, and he was a student at Rhode Island Community College, looking to transfer to U.R.I., Providence College, or maybe even Brown. He was from Providence but not Federal Hill, like I'd thought. He was working his way through school, working odd jobs, the reporter announces, and I brace myself, waiting for her to mention the dean's party, but she doesn't. They'll put it together eventually, I now realize.

I move the mouse to go read the article, but the clip isn't over yet. Another woman comes on, middle-aged, and a man. Danny's parents. She's crying, but the father is managing to keep it together, telling the reporter about his son, how he wanted to be a chef, own his own restaurant, be a successful business man. Then the old man loses it, and I start to feel dizzy, like I'm being sucked down to the bowels of hell.

A mouse click on the adjacent window, and I'm reading the accompanying article. It was a state park that night, and so the state police are involved too. They know he had sex that night, with a woman, no more than an hour before he died, and that she had B- blood. I'm sure there's more. It's not enough I tell myself. There are lots of women with B- blood.

I look it up. 1.5% of the population. And a feeling of dread comes over me. Then another feeling . . . that feeling that I'm being watched.

It's quiet now in the house. Even the dryer has stopped. My eyes focus on the basement door. It's ajar. The feeling intensifies, until I'm overwhelmed and consumed by it and I don't remember anything more.

8

"Emily!"

Hands on me, shaking.

"Emily!"

Eyes open, slowly. Horizontal, wet, on the floor. Green and white tiles. My dad's voice. "Emily!"

I realize now, I'm lying on the floor in the rec room, just like when I broke my arm. There's wet on my face and a bad smell. Vomit. I start to push myself up. There's just a little there on the floor and a little more coming out of my mouth and down my cheek. I can smell the alcohol, but I don't remember.

I push my hair back. Oh god, it's on my hand and in my hair too.

I don't know where my glasses are, but when I move my hand to reach for the black and glass sparkly blur, I hear the empty echo of a hollow bottle. Definitely not my specs. I have it halfway to my face when I see that it's a Jack Daniel's empty. God, I must have been desperate.

"Jesus, that bottle was almost full," my dad says, his voice full and almost breaking.

He reaches down and scoops me up. He's stronger than I remember. "Come on, let's get you upstairs."

I fight him off. "I can walk myself," I tell him, and he hesitates.

Finally half-letting go, he helps me to my feet. My laundry skirt is halfway up my stomach and I move to pull it down, almost losing my balance. I feel like I'm on Mars, zero gravity, then burning up, like I'm on the sun in a solar flare, going out in a blaze of glory.

My father helps me upstairs, arm around my waist, shoulder to shoulder, and I want to die. In my bedroom, still stuck together, I make my way to the bathroom, pushing him off as I close the door behind me, forcing him to let go, but making brief eye contact beforehand.

I pull off my clothes, as slowly as I can, every motion throbbing. It's everywhere, and it smells. Alcohol and gastric juice. On the sleeve of my green sweatshirt, down the side of my skirt, in my hair, and on my face. I see the tuna sandwich I had for lunch, and I'm ready to give it up again.

I turn on the shower and get in without even waiting for it to get warm. I need to wake up, be as sober as possible for when I have to face my father. The shame overwhelms me, and I sit at the bottom of the shower-tub under the cold water, head between my knees. By the time I get back up, the water's warmed a bit, and I rinse off before cleaning myself thoroughly with soap and shampoo.

I'm embarrassed to come out of the shower in a towel—even my underwear is soiled—but my dad isn't there. Just my pajamas, clean and laid out on the bed. My glasses are on top, and the rest of my laundry is folded there on the bed next to it.

It's dark out, and I look at the clock. 8:23. I'm still moving slowly but manage to slip into my pajamas and put my clean laundry on top of the dresser. I'm still figuring to go out and talk to my dad, but I realize I just don't have the strength for it. I'm still pretty drunk but half-hungover, and too tired to speak.

No, it's bedtime now. He's not expecting that inevitable conversation right now. Tomorrow. I remember to drink water, having two large glasses before I turn out the light.

"Stop drinking, Emily," I hear my old teacher tell me, as I fall asleep. But I can't, I want to go back and tell him. The door, and that feeling, and the dead boy with the crying parents . . . too much, too much for me to face sober, to face alone.

The next morning, I'm in better shape than I expect. I kept drinking water throughout the night, each time I had to get up to pee. It took care of the dehydration, and, of course, I hadn't mixed my drinks—just a straight, clean, whiskey high—so my hangover is light.

Still, I sleep till almost nine, more than twelve hours, and I feel okay. I take another shower. My jeans are downstairs where I hung them to dry, and I put on a pair of gold corduroys. They're a little easier to get into but still tight around my ass. Right now, that's the least of my problems.

I know my dad'll be downstairs, reading, either some French play or *The New York Times*. I gird myself to go and face him, when there's a knock on the door. I let him in, avoiding eye contact, until finally I look at him, eyes dark, like mine, fearful like mine. The shame and embarrassment almost overwhelm me, but at least I'm sober now. Then I start longing to be drunk again.

I realize the deal's probably blown now. I won't be graduating in December. Or maybe ever. It'll all come out, and I'll go into rehab or something horrible like that.

He sits on my bed, patting the spot next to him in a gesture of love and affection, and I join him. It's worse than I thought.

There, sitting hip-to-hip, he looks over at me. "What happened last night?"

And I start lying. "All the kids do it and I just wanted to try it to see what it was like and I had too much. I . . . I didn't know. God, I felt so sick. I'm an idiot."

The last part is certainly true.

His lips stay together, moving in a quick succession of expressions that I can't quite read until it becomes clear: emotion, strong and deep, then relief.

He puts his arm around me and pulls me in tight, like at the restaurant, but this time, it makes me feel terrible. "You're obviously not an experienced drinker," he says, smiling at me. His eyes sparkle, wet and glassy.

I lean into his shoulder. "I'm sorry, Daddy."

"It's okay, baby. Just don't do it again."

Unable to bear looking up at him, I bury my face in his arm. "No, I won't. Ever." I want it to be true, but I know it's a promise I can't keep.

"Well we won't talk about it any more then," he says, pushing me off just enough to meet my face and give me a smile. I force a smile back. I can't believe I'm not bawling, but the truth is, I don't know what I'm feeling, aside from the sheer terror that he'll find out. It would kill him. It would kill *me*.

He puts his hand to my head and strokes my hair. My mother used to do that too. I know they both love me, and without warning I'm ready to cry.

"This really is a pretty haircut, sweetie," he tells me, getting up to leave.

I want to thank him, but all I can manage is a smile, doing everything I can to keep it together until after he's gone. When he's out the door, I bury my face in the pillow and cry like a two-year old.

An hour later, I'm laying back on my bed, replaying the whole thing. I can't believe that's it. Caught red-handed, lying to his face, and he still doesn't know. I was sure he'd put it together, the bottles going down all those years . . . but he didn't, the perfect student, Ivy Leaguer, the perfect daughter weighing off against it all in his mind.

Still thinking about it, I go down to the rec room to get my jeans. I see the basement door, still ajar, and I start to get mad at myself. No one was down there. No one is stalking me. It's all in my alcohol-addled paranoid brain. Yes, the phone calls are creepy, but that's all they are, phone calls. *Fuck Steve.*

Danny comes back into my mind. I want to tell his parents, tell them what happened, how sorry I am, but he shouldn't have done what he did. I trusted him, and he hurt me. And now he's dead. I don't think I ever want to have sex again.

Walking back upstairs, jeans in hand, I think about the deal with my father. I've been given a huge reprieve. I don't want to blow it. I could still get caught. So I make another deal, a deal with myself. I'll stop drinking, go cold turkey, at least until I finish school and have my diploma in hand. If I do that, it'll be alright, I won't get caught, I tell myself.

I end up lying around all day like a cat, sitting on my fat ass watching TV. I feel okay but too hungover to go out for a run. My head's alright—a little fuzzy, a little tired—but it doesn't hurt. It's my stomach that's unsettled, and the thought of moving around too much or eating makes me want to chuck all over again. So I just drink as much water and Diet Coke as I can, pissing the booze out during the commercials. The downstairs bathroom is small—just a powder room between the kitchen and den—convenient, but not nearly as nice as my bathroom upstairs. I'm going to miss having my own bathroom when I get back to school.

My dad's been in and out all day, and when he comes in around 4:30, I'm watching *Jeannie* again. *Times* in hand, he sits down but doesn't start in on the paper, looking over by where my feet are perched up on the ottoman, and for a moment, I think he's noticed my "I Dream of Jeannie" toe-nails. But then I realize he's looking past them at the real McCoy there on the TV, perfect curves, bare midriff, and blond.

I watch him watching her. Can't blame him, really. She *is* beautiful. But it makes me feel sort of bad. Then he turns to me.

"Emmie," I love when he calls me that. It makes me feel safe and loved, and I forget about the blonde in the pink silk pants. "I thought maybe we'd go out and see a movie tonight."

It actually sounds like a great idea. I'm dying to get out of the house. My stomach is settling down, and I'm starting to get really hungry.

"Can we go to Chan's?" I ask him like I'm still ten. It's a local fast food place that has huge burgers with lots of onions and salty shoestring fries, and I miss it in Providence.

"Sure." He looks down at his watch. "Maybe in an hour or so?"

We have a brief discussion about what to see, my father voting for *Planet of the Apes* (He read the original novel, in French, of course) and me voting for *Once* (which I read in English), before settling on *Crazy, Stupid, Love.*

I get my burger with extra onions at Chan's and my father has his with sauce on the side. We share fries and rings.

He's eating slowly, and I can tell there's something on his mind.

"Em," he says, picking at an onion ring. "I thought we'd go to church on Sunday," he continues, "you know, before you go back."

Neither of my parents are terribly religious, but we used to go, regularly at first, then more sporadically after they got divorced. I didn't mind it. I believe in God and always had the feeling that going was good for me. Even Brown couldn't squeeze that out of me. But I get the feeling that my dad has an ulterior motive. Maybe he thinks I need it. Maybe I didn't fool him about the booze. Maybe it's just more paranoia.

Either way, I can't say no. "Okay," I tell him, not looking up.

"Good," he says.

My flight on Sunday doesn't leave until six, but it'll still be tight to go in the morning, come back and pack, and make the flight in Indianapolis, an hour away. But it's okay. It'll be fun, I tell myself. It's only a short walk away, and the building is beautiful. I always felt lucky to be Episcopalian. The best of both worlds, my grandfather would say, Catholic pomp and Protestant style. He was dead before I ever realized how sly he was being.

I'm thinking about it all through the movie, but it's out of my mind by the time we're back home. Brushing my teeth before bed, it hits me that it's almost time for me to head back to school. A pang hits me in the breastbone, and I miss my father, even though he's in the next room.

I go running again the next day, Saturday, finally getting a chance to blow off some steam. I weighed myself for the first time in months before I left the house. 132. I decide to start exercising regularly to get back down to 120. That and stop drinking. And get my act together with school. It's good to set goals.

I pick up the pace around the stadium. *Run that ass off!* I tell myself. By the time I get back, I feel like I need an oxygen tank, but I'll work up my endurance. In the meantime, a shower and a nap.

We go to the movies again on Saturday. It's the *Apes* this time, and I hate it, but I'm glad to make my dad happy. Somehow we end up at Denny's afterward, and he tells me all about the book. I wish I could read French better, and I tell him. Then my mother's name comes up—I'm not sure who mentioned her first—and my dad tells me she's getting an award from the National Academy in France. It makes me proud, even though I ache for my dad.

The French Academy, I think to myself, alone in bed, later. *Mom is pretty smart.* Then I start to think about what I'm going to wear to church tomorrow morning, my last day home, and I get sad all over again.

9

Looking through my closet, I narrow my choices down to two: The black pantsuit I brought with me or a blue and white skirt and jacket "sailorsuit" that my grandparents bought for me when I was in high school. I go back and forth, unable to make up my mind.

It's nice to wear a skirt to church, but then I have to shave my legs. I should also wear pantyhose, which I'm not sure I have. It also reminds me of that night, but I dismiss the thought. Maybe I should just wear the pantsuit. But the thing is, I just wore it a couple of days ago, and even though no one will notice, I hate wearing the same thing twice in a row like that. I finally try both outfits on. *Twice.*

The skirt is pleated and was always a little big, but now, twelve pounds later, it fits perfectly. I find a pair of cute shoes with buckles that I haven't worn in a dog's age, and they go perfectly. That cinches the deal. I find a pair of nude pantyhose in my sock drawer. Perfect.

I shave my legs in the shower, washing my hair and shaving under my arms in the process. Brushing my hair out afterward, I wonder how long the cut will last. Putting on my stockings, I notice there's a run. *Damn.* It may still be okay. It's at the top of the left thigh, and when I get them on, I can see that my skirt will cover it. Unless it runs even more. I'll have to risk it. I finish dressing and check myself out in the mirror. Suddenly, the sailor suit looks a little too much like it's for a kid, and I debate changing back into the black pants.

Then my father calls upstairs. It's after nine, and we're going to be late. "I'll be right down!" I yell. I stand for a moment in front of the mirror. Ugh. Torn stocking, sailor suit. I kind of want to change, but it's too late. A minute later, and we're heading out the door.

"You look pretty," my dad tells me. He's learning.

He's wearing a suit that makes him look like a professor, and I kind of wish he were wearing something better. A red tie with a brown jacket. Oh brother. I wish he'd asked me. Then again, I had enough trouble on my own.

The service is nice, and the minister gives a sermon on helping others, that is other people who you *don't* like. He discusses the passage about turning the other cheek, what it means, and how it's been misinterpreted. My mind wanders, and I don't really get the whole thing. All I can think is that I killed someone, and I'm going to burn in hell. I try to rationalize that it was self-defense, but I know it wasn't. I'll be good from now on, I say to myself, silently. I hope it's enough.

After the service, we mingle, and my dad introduces me to a woman. It's been so long since I've been here, I don't really know anyone anymore.

"Sharon, this is my daughter, Emily."

She smiles and squeezes my hand. "Sharon Glass."

She's pretty, and I can see that my dad likes her. So *that's* why he wanted to come today. I watch and listen to them talk for a minute. He brags about his Ph.D. from Yale and his daughter at Brown. She looks impressed. She's got on too much makeup, but she's tall and beautiful. She looks a little like my mother, but my mother is prettier. I'm guessing she's probably a few years younger than my dad, maybe forty, thin with a nice, form-fitting print dress.

I'm glad there's someone he likes. I think she likes him too. When we're walking back home, I mention her. "Sharon is very pretty, Dad," I say, being a little too obvious. "I like her."

He shoots me a glance out of the corners of his eyes. "Yes," he says, and I can tell he wanted my take on her and is glad that I like her. I really don't think there's been anyone since my mom. Gone almost eleven years, but she's a tough act to follow.

"Sharon. It's a pretty name," I say, probably adding one thing too many.

On the plane, several hours later, I think about them to-gether. *Don't get your hopes up, Emily*, I think to myself. The stewardess passes with the drink cart, and I hear the little bottles of gin and vodka clinking. *You've got your own life to get sorted out.*

10

My roommate is already in bed, asleep, when I get in. It's past eleven, and I'm exhausted. She's the last person I feel like talking to, and I'm extra careful not to wake her, but my suitcase falls over, and there we are having a conversation.

"You got your hair cut!"

"Yeah, something a little different," I say, pulling at it a little.

"It looks great."

I'm glad she said so, but it's been a week and I'm over it now.

She keeps talking, and *I'm* ready to fall over. Every boring detail of her boring spring break. She went to her aunt's in Woonsocket. Actually, her *great* aunt's. It just keeps getting better. She's a pre-med and spent the whole time studying for the MCATs. She wants to be a child psychiatrist. This is the longest conversation I've had with her since we've been roommates.

Finally, I open my suitcase and start to put my stuff away, eventually changing into my pajamas, but she doesn't get the hint. Then I excuse myself and go off to brush my teeth. I take as long as possible, and when I get back, there she is, sitting cross-legged on her bed, books out, studying!

"I can't go back to sleep," she tells me.

I don't even bother to smile at her, climbing into bed and turning the light off in my half of the room. Nine hours later, I'm sitting in medieval history, eyelids drooping.

It feels strange to be back in class. It always does the first day after break, and even some of the professors are a little lethargic. By the time astronomy rolls around, I'm over it, but I still don't want to go. *Tim.* I'm sure I'll have hear all about his spectacular break at Wisconsin Dells or some other horror. But then I get this feeling that he isn't going to be there. *If only.*

It would be a great class if he weren't. I love Professor Marsden, and we're still studying about stars, and, in particular, *our* star, the sun. I took this class on a whim, but I'm going to be sorry to see it end. Oh well, I won't think about it now. There's still another six weeks.

I come in just as the bells rings, and the class is quiet. Something feels a little off—Marsden is up in front of the class, sitting on his desk, looking down at his feet, bouncing the backs of his heels off the metal front. He's usually talking to the students right up until the bells rings, and he always starts class right on time. *First day after break*, I think. Even Professor M isn't immune.

He starts slowly. "I guess most of you have heard about Tim by now."

A stone sinks in the pit of my stomach, like I know what he's going to say next. Looking around, I finally notice that

Tim isn't here. And I feel like I knew that, like I knew it all along. *Tim is dead*, I think to myself.

Marsden continues, not quite getting to the point for another minute or two, then I see a copy of *The Brown Daily Herald* sticking out from the knapsack of the guy a row ahead of me and to the left. Dave somebody-or-other. There's Tim's face, crumpled under the masthead. The paper is rolled up, and I can't see the headline. I reach over and tap Dave on the shoulder.

"Can I take a peak at your paper?" I whisper when he turns around.

He looks at me for a second, hesitates, possibly taken aback at my insensitivity, then reaches in and hands it to me.

"I just want to see the story," I say by way of explanation, and he nods faintly.

And there's the headline: SOPHOMORE MISSING.

I read. He's twenty years old, from Wisconsin, hasn't been seen since the day before break. He was supposed to go home. His parents called the school then the police. They found his car, stripped and wrecked down at India Point, not too far from where I got my hair cut. *He's dead, he's dead*, I think. I *know*.

I feel the blood rush from my head, like I'm going to pass out, but no such luck. I'm still conscious, burning in my own skin. I need to leave. Now. Marsden's saying something about hoping for the best as I rise from my seat and run for the door. Out in the hallway, I make for the bathroom, but I stop outside the door, at the water fountain, hanging my head over it.

I don't really even want a drink. I don't know what I want, but there, hanging my head over the metal basin, my

breathing slows a bit. Still fast, but no longer hyperventilat-
ing. Then I feel a hand on my shoulder. I turn around.
Marsden.

We sit on the bench for a minute or two. "I'm okay," I
tell him. "No I'm not," I add a half-second later.

"You two were dating, right?" he says.

I move my eyes to the side in an abortive roll. "Well no,
not exactly," I say.

I'm not sure he gets it. "You were friends then," he says,
and I nod.

"Yeah, I guess so."

"They may still find him. He might be fine," he says.
"Just try to relax. Don't worry about class. Go home, rest.
Come see me in my office tomorrow. I'll fill you in on what
you missed."

"Thank you," I say, realizing I'm going to have to go
back in for my backpack.

It must've shown on my face. "Wait here, I'll bring your
stuff out."

A minute later, he's there with my backpack. I notice the
hair on the backs of his fingers, dark like his beard, as he
hands it to me. He's wearing a wedding ring, and it makes me
think how lucky his wife is, as I take the strap and walk away.

I fidget around my room like a caged animal, too per-
turbed to even want a drink. Then, suddenly, the idea is in
my head. No, no booze. I promised myself. A deal's a deal.
Then I get the idea to go for a run. Yeah, a run. Work my fat
butt off. I promised myself that too. I'm suited up and on
my way before the craving comes back, but by then I have it
under control. I run up towards the athletic center, away

from India Point, then around Brown Stadium to Blackstone Boulevard.

It's warm out, and by the time I'm back, my t-shirt is soaked. I take a long shower, get dressed, and go for a walk. It's dinner time, but I have no appetite. Walking up Hope Street, I criss-cross the campus, hitting all the major quads on the way back—Pembroke, Wriston, the College Green.

I try to remember the last week before break, but I can't. I can't even seem to remember the last time I saw Tim. I stop in the computer center to log on and read my email. Tim's email! I remember now. He sent an email. I can't remember the exact date as I look for it frantically in my inbox. And then I remember that I deleted it. I double check to see if it's in my deleted items folder, but it's not. I emptied that too.

Then I check the *ProJo* to see if there's anything more about Danny. Tim and Danny. Two boys I knew, one dead and one missing, probably also dead. A nervous, almost panic-stricken laugh escapes from my mouth, and the girl at the computer in front of me, turns around. I avoid her eyes.

There's nothing new on Danny, and I figure that's probably good. I sleepwalk through the next day, realizing too late that I missed my appointment with Professor Marsden. I hate myself. I pick up the campus phone and call him.

"Hello, Professor Marsden?"

"Emily?"

I can't believe he recognizes my voice.

He continues even before I have a chance to offer an explanation. "You forgot to come by today, huh?"

"Yeah."

"Well, don't worry about it. I know you're a little preoccupied." He pauses for a second. "I'd really like to give you the notes before class tomorrow."

"That would be great," I say, relieved that he's not mad at me.

"Why don't you come by tonight. After dinner. We're in the R.D.'s suite in Greene Hall."

"You mean your house?"

"Yeah, stop by, and I'll give you the notes. I should be back by six. If not, my wife'll let you in."

"Okay, thanks," I say, wanting to get off the phone before he changes his mind.

So I'm going to get to meet *Mrs.* Marsden, see where they live. Greene Hall. A married couple getting stuck in a crummy dorm, having to babysit a bunch of spoiled college kids. At least my parents never had to do that.

I grab a peanut butter sandwich at the refectory and head over to Greene. I look down at myself. I'm wearing a pair of green corduroys and a long, unbuttoned sweater over a yellow shirt. It doesn't matter, but I kind of feel like I should be dressed decently when I go over to my professor's house. But it's five of six, so this is going to have to be good enough.

A boy starts talking to me as I walk down the hall. "You know what this is for?" he asks, holding up what looks like some strange piece of lab equipment.

"No," I say, speeding by. He's about to say something else, trying to engage me, but I look over and cut him off. "Sorry, I'm in kind of a hurry."

Then he and his friend start laughing. Freshman, no doubt. Doors open, kids hanging out, studying, talking. No, I don't envy Marsden having to deal with this.

Reaching his door at the end of the hall, I knock, and a petite woman with small brown eyes and dark wavy hair parted in the middle answers. "Emily?"

I smile and she flashes a big smile back, standing aside and waving me in. She's mousey but pretty with a great smile and perfect teeth. She offers me cookies, and I tell her I'm trying to lose weight. She does a friendly half eye roll, reaching out and touching my arm. "You don't need to lose any weight." Easy for her to say in her size two jeans. But I know she's just trying to be nice. And I think she might even mean it. I try to imagine myself as slim as she is.

She leads me into the living room. The apartment is bigger than I had imagined. Then again, in my mind I was comparing it to a dorm room, and it *is* a real apartment—bedroom, living room, dining room, and kitchen. I sit on the couch in the living room, wondering how long I'm going to have to wait. I'm not good in social situations, and even though Mrs. M seems nice, I just want to get the notes and go.

"I'm Diane, by the way," she says to me, extending her hand. "I'll go get Bill."

Bill and Diane. Makes me think of Bob and Celia. *I hope your marriage works out better than my parents' did.* At any rate, I'm glad *Bill* is here, so I don't have to sit around making small talk with *Diane.* I hate that.

Looking around, I have a sudden sense of urgency to take the place in. Once she gets Bill, I'll get the notes and go, losing the opportunity. And who knows when I'll get another.

It's a warm room, funky, not quite adult but way past college. The couch is velvet, light green, and my corduroys catch on the cushion. There's a Persian rug and Middle-Eastern-looking tea set bushed in amongst the books on the other side. The coffee table looks used, dark wood, scuffed up, with a couple of drink ring stains, but solid.

There's a reproduction Rembrandt over the fireplace. A fireplace! Nice! And a poster from an art exhibit at the Prado in Madrid. I decide that Bill and Diane are a fun couple, probably a lot more fun than Bob and Celia were. But that was probably Celia's fault.

I'm grinning, thinking about them all—Bob, and Celia, Bill, and Diane—when Bill walks in, and I revert back to the fifth-year college student.

"Hi, Professor Marsden."

He gives me the notes, taking the time to explain them to me, practically recreating the lecture. A situation like this can get toxic fast—boring, awkward, impossible to escape, but this is the opposite, and a half hour later, Mrs. M and I are sitting on the couch, hanging on every word.

When he finishes telling us about the nuclear fusion reactions that fuel the sun, I have a ton of questions, but I don't want to impose. But my face gives me away, and I'm busted.

"Questions?" he asks, looking right at me.

"All those nuclear reactions . . . isn't it going to explode?" I blurt out.

"No, not for millions of years."

"Well *that's* good!" I say, and I hear Mrs. M slap her thighs, starting to rise from the couch, and the spell is broken.

I get up too, and we look at each other for a moment. I can see how enraptured she was by her husband's talk, and I can tell how much she loves him. I'm about to go, when she asks if I'm alright. I guess her husband told her about my little episode. I tell them both that I'm doing okay.

Twenty minutes later, the three of us are still standing and talking. I tell them about my academic situation, that I'm switching my concentration back to biology, but that I wish I could switch to astronomy. I tell them I'm trying to get a job in the Bio Lab, and Mrs. M asks which one. Then I spot the row of biology journals on the near shelf.

"The Sleep Lab," I tell her.

"Oh, Boxner's lab!" she says, coming alive. Then she looks at me. "You know, he's leaving."

"Really?"

"Yeah, he's going to be the new dean of the medical school."

"That's great," I say for no particular reason. I don't know Boxner from a hole in the wall. I didn't even interview him for the story I did in the school paper.

"And you know who's taking over the lab?" She gestures at herself, and my mouth opens a little in surprise.

"You?"

She nods, smiling.

"Wow! Really?" This time I really *am* surprised. I figured she worked for the school, but I had no idea she was on faculty in the bio department.

"Yeah," she says, grinning slyly. "I'll put in a good word for you."

"That's great!" I say, unable to hide my enthusiasm.

She tells me she can't promise me anything—they already have a bunch of applicants—but if I'm willing to stay the summer, I'd have a good chance. *Perfect*. It's kismet, I tell myself, a sign from God. It's all going to work out. *Just stop drinking and take care of yourself.*

I hug her on the way out, and she hugs me back. She's a warm person, something I miss. I feel like running back and telling my roommate, but I don't want to give her any ideas.

Danny and Tim are still gone, but there's nothing I can do about that. It's bad, I know, but I'll be good from now on. Clean and sober. Maybe I'll win a Nobel Prize or something. I'll send in my official application tomorrow.

I'm still thinking about it days later, waiting to hear if I'm in or not. Maybe I could do it without the lab gig, taking the waitress job downtown, squeezing in an extra couple of courses, but this would definitely make things much smoother and easier. Then I get the letter in my mailbox at the student center. I'm in. In! Still holding the letter, I pick up a copy of the paper and sit down in the lounge to read it.

Tim is still missing, and the trail has grown cold on Danny Marcone, and I feel it all coming together. The police aren't going to figure it out, I tell myself. And they're losing interest. And me? I'm just another student, finishing up the year and getting ready for summer. I've already got a job lined up, assistant techie in the Sleep Lab. It'll look great on my résumé.

11

I finish up the school year without event. I even manage to pull off a 4.0. Not a drop of booze, and I'm feeling good. I've settled into a routine, running every afternoon, staying away from anything sweet. I've lost three pounds in six weeks, and I'm down to 129. I weigh myself everyday, stopping in at the gym on my run. My jeans are still tight, but a guy yelled something obscene at me when I was running the other day. It frightened me a little, but at least someone's noticing.

I got my hair cut again. I'm sick of wearing glasses, but I've gotten used to it. It's senior week now, and my new job starts in less than a week. I need to find a new place to live, and I haven't even started to look yet.

It's hot out, and I'm laying back on my bed in a summer dress with the window open and the drapes shut. My exams are over, and I have nothing to do. It's the first really hot day, and I'm feeling lazy. I even left my shoes on. Plain, black loafer pumps. Looking down at them, I think that they're kind of ugly. I should put on sandals, but I'd need to re-do my toenails first, and I don't feel like it.

Campus Dance is tonight, and graduation is in a few days. People who entered after me will be graduating, and I'm still here, half a year away. *If* everything works out okay. It bothers me, but I try not to let it. Campus Dance bugs me too. I've been here five years, and I've never gone. I didn't really want to go at first, but now I feel like I'm the only person on campus who's missing out on all the fun.

The phone rings.

I jump up in a start. It happens every time the phone rings since I've been back. Even though I haven't heard from my heavy-breathing stalker, even though I'm pretty sure I'm free and clear. The police wouldn't call, I tell myself.

"Hello?"

"Hi, Emily. This is Professor Sinclair."

It takes me a second. "Oh, Diane!" I say.

"Yes," she says, a little reserved, and I realize my faux pas.

"I'm sorry, Professor Sinclair, I forgot that you use your maiden name."

"It's okay. You can call me Diane when you're over the apartment, just not in the lab."

I get it. I'm working for her now. "Yeah, sure, of course, no problem."

"I thought maybe you could come over to the lab, meet everyone. I've got some paperwork for you to fill out."

"Yeah, when should I come by?"

"You busy now?

"I'll be right over."

I don't really feel like going, but it'll be good to get out. Reaching for my brush, I realize how sweaty I am. I already showered today, but I could use another one. I'll wait until after my run. A quick dab of antiperspirant will do the trick in the meantime, then I realize I'm out.

My roomate's probably got some extra—always prepared for everything. It grosses me out a little bit to have my hand in there, but fumbling through her drawer, I find it buried under her underwear. Pulling it out, I stare . . . no, wait, something's not right. I drop it back into the drawer in horror. A dildo! Jesus Christ! I push a pair of her panties back over it with the tip of one finger.

Running into the bathroom holding my hand out, I wash it with hot water for the next five minutes, then I start laughing. *I guess all work and no play makes Jill a dull girl.* They keep coming into my head. *I'm glad to see she has a hobby.*

I'm thinking about it all the way to the quad, grinning. I knew lots of women did that, I just didn't think she would be one of them. It's a disgusting habit, something I'd never do myself, but it makes her seem more human and less unlikable to me. *She needs a boyfriend*, I think to myself.

When I get to the lab, my amusement has dimmed, but just a little. Popping my head in, the place looks empty. Then I see someone off in the back. It's a guy, looks like an undergrad, probably the other techie. I knew there was another one who'd already been working here for a semester. He looks up.

"Are you Emily?"

He's thin and very pale, with dusty blond hair and blue eyes. He doesn't smile and seems very serious.

"Yes," I say, every bit the geek that he is.

There's an awkward moment where we could shake hands or something but don't. I wait for him to introduce

himself, but there's just silence. So I smile a little at his ob-
tuseness, moving my face forward and opening my eyes
wider to prompt him. He reacts with a slightly puzzled look,
which makes me think he's sort of cute, and I finally ask, a
little silly and exaggerated, in a teasing way, like I was talking
to a kid.

"And what's your name?"

"Oh. Uh. I'm Adam," he says, wiping his hand on his lab
coat, as if finally ready to shake hands, but we still don't.

And I thought *I* was awkward!

"Is Professor Sinclair here?" I ask.

"Yeah," he says, coming to life, turning to his right and
pointing to a door on the opposite wall, "through the door
then first office on the right." Then, after a moment of
thought, he adds, "Short lady with brown hair."

"Yes, I know, we've met before," I tell him with a little
playful sarcasm. It's nice to be the coolest person in the
room for a change.

I go over to the door and look back to ask about summer ID validation, when I see that he's already looking at me.
He looks away quickly, and I decide against it. Was he checking me out? I think he might have been checking me out. I
look down at myself. Maybe he was looking at my legs. I *have*
been running. Maybe I shouldn't be so surprised, but I am,
and it makes me feel good.

I spend the next half hour with Professor Sinclair. She
seems glad to see me, but she's all business, nothing like the
woman I met at the apartment when I came to get the notes
that time.

She gives me a W-2 form and signs my registration card
so I can get credit: Bio 297, Reading and Research, 4 credits.

Awesome, I think to myself. Then I sit down with her, and she tells me about the lab, the study she's doing, the project.

There are electrodes and rats, and I remember why I quit bio, though it does sound kind of interesting. She's studying how light affects sleeping patterns in mammals, with rats standing in for people. If they only knew.

Different kinds of rats—white, brown, black, and gray; young, old, and in between; male and female. And different kinds of light—natural, artificial, fluorescent, and incandescent.

"We measure weight, size, and brain wave activity," she tells me. "Other things too: appetite, growth, sexual drive, teeth, and coat." She continues without looking up. "It's all in the lab book."

I can't stand vermin, and I'm incredibly relieved when she tells me that my job is to "accumulate and crunch data." Apparently that 'A' I got in my C++ programming class two years ago makes me the resident computer expert—or grunt, depending on how you look at it.

Mostly, I'll be getting lots of numbers and feeding them into someone else's programs to ferret out all the statistical correlations. I realize pretty quickly that this is actually the lowest level of work in the lab. They don't even trust me enough to feed the rats. But I don't care. It's better than waiting tables downtown, and I'm getting credit.

She takes me back out for the grand tour. I meet the rats, bristling when I hear the name Willie. Adam tags along, taking a sudden interest, and Sinclair seems to notice. She looks like she's about to say something to him, like 'get back to work,' but she doesn't. It would embarrass him, and she's too nice for that. I decide I still like her.

"I know you're supposed to start next week," she tells me. "But you think you could start tomorrow?" There's a pause. "I know it's short notice, and you can say no."

"Yeah, I can start tomorrow," I tell her.

An extra week's pay, I think.

"Great," she says, putting her hand on my shoulder and giving me a smile.

A moment later, and she's gone.

I look around the lab then quickly at Adam. "Bye," I say. "See you tomorrow."

A slight flash of panic crosses his face. He looks around, eyes darting, before they finally bolt to his watch.

"I was going to go for dinner soon. Want to go get something to eat? I mean if you're not busy."

Yeah, he was definitely checking me out. And I guess he must've liked what he saw. He is sort of cute, but I don't really want a boyfriend, and I don't want to get involved with someone I'm working with. Plus he is a bit of a geek. Even for me. But maybe he's just being friendly. I mean, if this is a date, the answer is *definitely* no. Been there, done that. But now, I'm not sure whether he's just being friendly or not. Either way, I decide I don't feel like it.

"No, thanks," I say.

I'm about to leave but I stand there for a moment longer. The windows are open, and the breeze is nice. The wind is punctuated by a low rumble. It's subtle at first but then unmistakable. The sound of a tuba.

We look at each other, and I crack a smile first. "Is that a tuba?" I ask.

He nods quickly. "Yeah. I used to play tuba in my high school band."

I'm not surprised.

"They're warming up for Campus Dance tonight," he tells me, walking over to the window and looking out.

I follow him and look out over the quad to see the Brown Band walking across the grass to set up on a makeshift stage. The tuba player—a big fat guy planted inside his instrument was taking a few random toots.

"I always wanted to go to Campus Dance," Adam tells me. "Maybe next year. I'll be a senior. I *should* go."

Me too, I think.

Taking the room in, side to side, a thought enters my mind. It's the top floor of the building, in the middle of the south side of the quad. The lab is the last room at the end and runs the width of the building, facing the inside of the quad on one side and the street on the other.

"If we stayed here until after the dance started, couldn't we just go out into the quad?"

He smiles for the first time, and his whole face lights up. He nods. "Yeah. They lock the doors at five, but they're locked from the *inside*." We both have mischievous grins now. "We could totally crash."

"What time is it?" I ask.

He rolls his head back in disappointment. "It's already past five. The doors are locked."

I get it. Once we leave the building, we can't get back in. So we can't go back home to change.

Silence for a second. I'm not really dressed for it, I think, moving my eyes down over my outfit. Well, at least I'm wearing a dress. I *could* get away with it.

I look over at Adam. Jeans, sneakers, and a plain t-shirt with a pocket. That's not going to cut it. Looking around, I spot the lab coat hanging on the back of his chair. I walk over and pull it off.

"Put this on," I tell him, and I help him into it.

I straighten it out on him, stand back and look. "It sort of looks like a Nehru jacket." I nod with him there standing still like a stuffed hominid at the Museum of Natural History. "Turn around."

He turns, one way then the other, arms out, exaggerated, being a little silly, and it makes me laugh, but the lab jacket is actually working.

"Yeah, you could totally get away with this."

12

We hang around the lab for another hour, until after Diane leaves. I didn't want her to see me there, hanging out, distracting her other techie, but she gives me a big smile on her way out. I'm sure she thinks we look "cute" together. Ugh. She should stick to breeding rats.

We both relax a little after she leaves. He tells me all about himself—another valedictorian, plus a Westinghouse Science Prize winner, and National Merit Scholar. His dad works for the NIH, and his mother is a housewife. He's got an older sister who's a writer working for *The Village Voice* in New York. And he definitely likes me.

I like him too, at least so far, but I'm just not interested in that way. I tell him I'm 23; I've already been here for five years; that my parents are divorced; and that I'm from Indiana. That ought to scare him off! But it doesn't seem to.

It's almost seven before we finally decide to head out. A quick pit stop, but I don't even have lipstick to put on. I almost never wear it but figure it might help. Checking myself out in the mirror, I notice the back of my dress is wrinkled from all the sitting, and I try to straighten it out without much success. I wish I had taken that second shower. Oh well. At least my hair looks okay.

Adam leads the way out onto the quad. It's dusk, and there's a pretty good crowd, mixed, alumni, faculty, and students. I notice how adult some of the students look, all dressed up in stockings and suits, and I feel shabby in my casual cotton dress. Even the staff is dressed better than we are, but no one seems to care. Noticing a waiter who looks like Danny, I think of him for a moment then shove it out of my mind. I'm hungry.

Adam brings me a plate of food. So he got me to have dinner with him after all. It's a little greasy, but the stuffed mushroom caps are really good, and I send him back for more. I notice a wet bar over in the corner, by the steps to the student center, and I have to fight myself to not have a drink.

When Adam comes back, he sees me staring and grins. "Want to get us something to drink?"

I look up at him, still holding the plate of mushrooms. "Huh?"

"You're 23, right?" he says. "You could get us a couple of drinks."

"I don't have my ID," I tell him, and it's true. I hadn't thought of it before, but I *can't* get us anything to drink.

He shrugs. "I don't really drink anyway."

"Me neither," I tell him, my mouth already full.

With *that* possibility removed, we walk around and check out the festivities. The band is pretty good, and it's fun to watch everyone dancing. But I don't want to join them.

And the uneasy suspicion that he's going to ask me creeps into my head.

He finally breaks the tension. "I'd ask you to dance, but I don't really know how." Then he furls his eyebrows, more serious for a second. "To dance that is."

Yes, I get it. "Me neither, I say," leaving it at that.

Continuing around the inside of the quad, I spot Diane—Professor Sinclair—and then, a second later, Professor Marsden. I point them out to Adam. She looks beautiful, in a black strapless chiffon dress, and he's all decked out in a tuxedo. She sits in his lap, puts her arm around him, and kisses him, and I feel a twinge of envy.

"Come on, let's get out of here," I tell Adam, but he's one step ahead of me. I guess he doesn't want her to see us here either, though I'm not quite sure why. Then I realize it's just the awkwardness of the situation, his and mine. The crummy clothes and purloined lab coat aren't helping.

Going back to the adjacent side of the quad, we sit up on the brick wall in front of the student center and look out over the crowd.

"Want something else to eat?" he asks.

I look over at him and smile. It's sweet of him to ask, and I appreciate it. "No thanks."

Looking out over the party, I feel a sense of serenity, almost happiness. I'm glad it worked out with the lab. I'm glad Adam is the other techie. We sit for a long while, talking sporadically, joking about the Brown Band and the overweight tuba player. It turns out Adam is a runner. I'm not surprised, he's very thin. I refrain from telling him that I've been running too—he might ask me to go with him, and I don't want to. Maybe when I lose a few more pounds.

Even though we haven't even danced, I'm really enjoying myself. In fact, I don't want to move, but I have to go to the bathroom. Finally, I excuse myself and head into the student center. It's crowded with students, boys and girls, holding hands, talking, gathering by the lounge area and in front of the vending machines. There are a bunch of girls pushing into the bathroom. It's co-ed at the student center. I never liked that, but after five years, I've gotten over it.

There are guys straightening their ties and girls putting on lipstick in front of the mirror as I make my way back out again, dressed like a cleaning woman. At least it feels that way. Then I see it. A couple making out in one of the over-sized chairs. She's wearing the same kind of chiffon dress as Diane, and for a second I think it might be her, but this woman has blond hair.

When I get closer, I see the side of her face out of the corner of my eye. It's my roommate, Jill. And she's making out with like the best looking guy in my astronomy class. I can't even believe it. I feel sick to the pit of my stomach. Jill. Jill with that disgusting dildo. And Mike the guy from my astronomy class. Even *she* has someone. I guess *I'm* the one who needs the boyfriend.

Adam and I leave a little while later. Back in my room, alone, I'm replaying the evening, thinking about Diane and Bill and Jill, her dildo, and Mike. I'm jealous. I admit it. But I still had a great time, and I'm glad I went. Maybe I do need a boyfriend. I wonder how Adam would be. I fall asleep thinking about it.

13

When I wake up, Jill still isn't back yet. *Good for her.* I force myself to say it out loud. It's eight o'clock in the morning, and I have to get ready for my first official day at the lab. It's Monday; graduation is tomorrow, and the campus will clear out pretty quickly after that. It'll be a ghost town by Wednesday afternoon and for about a week after that, until the summer students show up. And I still need to find a new place to live. It's May 23rd, and I have to be out by June 1st. I know I've left it to the last minute, but I could always stay in the dorm for the summer. The problem is that it'll be twice as expensive as a summer sublet, and I can't afford it.

I take a shower and put on my jeans and a nice, white short-sleeve blouse. Still tight, I think to myself, putting my hand on my butt. I shouldn't have had that second plate of those greasy mushrooms last night. But they were so good. I decide to skip breakfast.

I get to the lab a few minutes before nine, and both Adam and Professor Sinclair are already there.

"I'm not late am I?" I ask, whispering to Adam out of earshot of Diane, visible at her desk through the open door.

He nods vigorously. Then I see his eyes take me in. *Oh well. This is it, buddy, like it or not.* I walk over to Sinclair and, looking back, catch him staring at me again, wide-eyed, like a puppy dog who wants to be fed. I guess my fat ass isn't scaring him off so fast, and I'm kind of glad. I smile at him, and he blushes. I have to bite my tongue to stop from letting out a chuckle as I turn back towards the professor's office.

An hour later, and I'm set up at a workstation next to Adam. I don't need one, but I put on a lab coat—one of the longer non-Nehru ones. They have the air conditioning up all the way in here, and it's cold. Besides, it makes me feel more official, there in the lab with the regulation "uniform."

The work is a little dull, but I don't mind it. I figure out pretty quickly how to streamline the process of inputting and analyzing data using macros. I like programming, and Excel is easy to use.

When Adam asks if I want to go to lunch, I say yes. It's just take-out, sandwiches brought back to the lab from a place on Thayer Street, but it's nice to get out and walk. It feels like it's 90 degrees out, even though I know it's a bit less. The humidity is even worse than Indiana.

He's telling me he likes the meatball sub, but it's too hot, and we decide to split a large tuna. It's nice inside the shop—air conditioned but not too cold—and we decide to eat in. He asks me about running, and I don't want to put him off, but I'm not quite ready to let him see me in shorts, when I get the impression that that's *exactly* what he wants.

"I usually run in the late afternoon," I tell him.

"Yeah, me too," he says. We each take a bite of our half sub. He swallows first and continues. "Where do you live?"

I push the bite down and answer. "Funny you should ask. I'm in Harkness, but I've go to be out by next week."

"You need a place to live?" he asks, excited.

"Well yeah, sort of," I say, a little reluctant.

"One of our roommates is moving out, A. J., he's graduating, and we need a third person."

It's probably perfect, but I'm not ready for this either.

He seems to sense my hesitancy. "Well if you're interested, stop by this afternoon. It's on Pitman Street, number 24, between Ives and Gano." He takes another bite, and there's silence while he chews and swallows a gulp of Pepsi. "I won't be there this afternoon; I have to go downtown to pick up a package from my mom, but Jen will be there, and she'll show you around. I'll send her an email," he tells me. "You know, if you're interested."

Jen. Who the hell is Jen? "Is that your roommate?" I ask.

"Yeah, Jennifer."

A guy and a girl. And suddenly, I'm back on earth. That might actually be okay. Advantageous even.

"How much is the rent?"

"Nine hundred a month," he tells me, and my heart sinks. "Split three ways," he adds, and he's got me. Unless Jen is a psycho or the place is a hovel, I'm in—it's less than a third of what the dorm would cost and a little more than half what I had budgeted.

We finish our lunch and head back to the lab. It's almost too hot out to bear, and when we get back inside, it feels like we're entering a refrigerator.

"Is there any way we can turn the A.C. down?" I whisper to Adam.

He shakes his head. "No, the rats like it cold," he grins. "Built-in fur coat and all."

I don't know why, but I laugh. I mean, it's kind of gross, but *he* seems pretty amused by it, and I like his smile. I put my lab coat back on and go back to work.

I finish out the day and head home. Somehow, it's gotten even more humid, and I feel gross in my jeans. So I go running, take another shower, and change into a skirt.

It's late afternoon by the time I head over to the place on Pitman Street. The house is big—three stories—but kind of plain, with cheap plastic, fake wood siding. It's white. I wonder what his roommate is like.

I walk up the steps and notice two buzzers, one for each door, and a cardboard sign pointing around the back for apartment C, the one I'm looking for. Looking up, I take in the top floor, crowned by a cruciform pitched roof as I walk back down the stairs and up the driveway to the back of the house. I push the back buzzer, and a moment later there's a voice from above. A girl's head poking out from the gable on the top floor.

"Emily?" She's blond and gorgeous and smiling, and I'm feeling darker and uglier than ever. "It's unlocked."

Climbing the steps, I notice just how non-descript the place is. Linoleum and fresh paint, in multiple coats, indicating age, but none of the charm and flourish of an older house. It's multi-family, probably built in the '40s, I think to myself. Cheap, postwar, now filled with students. I'm finally getting some use out of that American Civilization survey course I took as a freshman.

The sweat is dripping off me by the time I reach the top, and there she is.

"Hi, I'm Jennifer," she tells me, sticking out her hand to shake.

She's even more beautiful up close, soft blond curls, clear, white skin, and a big warm smile, punctuated with a set of perfect teeth and full red lips. I feel like dropping to the ground and sticking up a white flag.

I force a smile and shake her hand. Even her hands are nicer than mine.

Leading me into the apartment, she talks to me back over her shoulder. She's so well put together and has such a cute figure that I'm barely listening. She's taller than I am—maybe 5′7—and is wearing a blue pants suit.

"So this is the living room," she says.

There's a drab fabric love seat in faded gold, a TV in the opposite corner, and an overstuffed and over worn chair on the side wall. I notice a couple of bio books on the floor.

"Are you a bio major too?" I ask.

She shakes her head. "I'm in the medical program," she tells me.

Right. The eight-year combined B.S./M.D. program. Just about impossible to get into. "That's great," I say, wanting to hate her more than ever.

She looks over at me, a little serious. "I almost flunked out my freshman year. It was *so* much work, and I started to go to too many parties, you know, drinking and everything." She shakes her head, suddenly much more sympathetic. "Anyway, I didn't, so here I am."

Me too, I think. And for a second, I want to tell her.

She takes me through the rest of the apartment—three bedrooms, one narrow bathroom under the east gable, and a large central kitchen. It's old and utterly lacking in charm, but it's cheap, totally functional, and seems safe.

Her bedroom is the nicest of the three, with a big closet and a nice view of the street. Her bed isn't made, but it's still neat. Adam's bedroom is bigger but not as well laid out. But it's also the only one that connects directly to the bathroom. "Just remember to lock both doors," she tells me.

The third bedroom, the one in the back, is smaller with a slightly lower ceiling, because of the pitched roof, but I like it the best—I'm shorter than either of the other two, so I don't mind the height, and being in the back, the room is quieter.

When we've come full circle, she puts her hands on her hips, as if to say *well, what do you think?*

I nod. "I like it."

I look at her. She has big green eyes. They're striking, and I want to tell her, but that would be weird. I still haven't decided whether I like her or not.

She seems to sense my hesitancy. "You know, I'm hardly ever here," she announces. "I practically live at my boyfriend's place. When I'm not at the hospital."

My body relaxes as soon as the words are out of her mouth. *She's got a boyfriend. And, she's not even here much.* I tell her I'll take it and excuse myself to use the bathroom.

"Great!" she says, smiling, hands still on her hips. "Don't forget to lock both doors, she tells me," repeating herself. It's the first thing I do when I get inside.

I'm relieved that it's actually clean. Jen, I figure. Boys are the worst. I'll probably have to take over the cleaning once I move in. I run the water so she won't hear me pee.

Finishing, I pull up my underwear, straighten myself out, and give in to my compulsion to search their medicine cabinet. I catch a glimpse of myself in the mirror. I know she's prettier than I am, but I like my face. Looking over the contents, shelf by shelf, I find a pair of nail scissors, an eyelash curler, a sample-sized tube of Crest, clear nail polish, shaving cream, a razor, and two toenail clippers. I'm simultaneously disappointed and glad. *No anti-fungal cream*, I think, smiling at myself in the mirror.

I close the cabinet just as I hear the apartment door open and Adam's voice muffling through the thin walls and closed door. Jen answers. I can't hear what they're saying, but he's obviously back from getting his package at the post office downtown. Looking down, I remember to flush, then I wash my hands and open the door. Stepping back into the kitchen, I see Adam and smile at him. "Hi."

He always seems a little stunned when he sees me, and I can't understand why, but he finally greets me back. "You want to watch Seinfeld?" he asks, heading into the living room carrying a bowl of cereal.

"No, I have to get back," I tell him, starting towards the door.

But a hand has me by the shoulder, gentle, from behind, stopping me. I turn my head back in surprise. *Jen.*

"Don't move," she tells me, in not quite a whisper.

I stand, mystified and slightly annoyed. Then I feel her other hand gently touch my backside and then something else. The brush of fabric against my butt as she pulls my skirt out of the waistband of my panties.

"Oh my God," I whisper back at her with a smile, realizing what had happened. "Thank you."

She smiles. "Don't mention it."

I instinctively reach around to make sure that my skirt is, indeed, where it is supposed to be. I'm sure I'm blushing, but I try to act as cool as possible heading to the door.

"You sure you don't want to stay for dinner?" Adam asks, looking over at me, never realizing the show he almost got to see.

"No," I tell him, really wanting to go now.

"Are you okay?" he asks, furling his eyebrows in that cute little way he has. "You look like you have heat stoke or something."

I'm blushing, you idiot! I think to myself. "It's just the light," I tell him, continuing on my way through the door.

14

I move in that weekend. Jen and Adam and Jen's boyfriend, Ted, help. I don't have much stuff, but I'm grateful to not have to move it all alone. Ted is much more average-looking than I expect—about 5′9, with thinning hair, even though he's young, but he's got a funny, lively personality, and we all seem to get along well.

By this time, I've decided I like Jen. And it's more than just the bit with the underwear. She's onto the whole thing between Adam and me and seems intent on helping to make it happen. She hasn't quite said it out loud to me, but I can tell. And I decide I want it to happen too. It would be nice to have a boyfriend, even if it's just a summer fling, and Adam really is a catch, smart and cute with nice eyes, even if a bit geeky. Who am I to judge on that count? I decide I like geeky.

The trouble is, neither of us seems to know quite how to make it happen. The first week is the worst. Walking in and out of the bathroom in a towel, I can only imagine what he thinks. I decide to buy a bathrobe, but then I wonder what signal that will send, and decide against it. Then again, what signal am I sending now? What signal do I want to send? When I see that there's a sale at Filene's Basement, I go down and get myself a nice, blue, terrycloth robe.

Meanwhile, he forgets to lock the bathroom door, and I walk in on him . . . shaving. Thank God. Then there's work. It's actually more relaxed there. We chat—maybe a little too much—and have lunch together everyday. By the second week, everything seems to have fallen into a rut.

Jen stops by on Sunday to get some clothes, and she pulls me aside into her room, sitting us both down on her bed, now made. "So?"

"What?" I ask, like I don't know, and she makes a face at me.

"How's it going with Adam?" She asks in a way that's intensely interested and impatient, and I begin to realize that even though I don't have a boyfriend *yet*, I may actually have my first real *girlfriend*.

It's a good feeling, but it also fills me with a sense of loss for what I've been missing out on for like my whole life. Except for Steve, I've hardly ever had *any* friends.

"We have lunch together," I tell her, immediately feeling like an idiot.

"Yeah?" she asks like a high school girl, slightly giddy, scooting closer to me on the bed, wanting more, but I just shrug, and she realizes that I've got nothing else. But then she gets a mischievous look in her eye, and she takes my hand, eyes widening. "We'll go out on a double date, the four of us."

I shift my eyes back and forth, unsure, and she pats my hand. "We just won't *tell* him it's a date. I'll send out an email.

We'll get some dinner, go to the Cable Car." She grins, jostling her shoulders a little. "You know, get close."

It's actually a pretty good idea. The Cable Car . . . I've only been there once or twice. It's a movie theater that shows old-time films, but instead of regular movie theater seating, it has rows of old, comfy couches and love seats. It's supposed to be a sort of make-out spot.

"What's playing?" I ask.

She rolls her eyes. "It doesn't matter!" Then she reaches for her phone. "I'll check," she says, like she's humoring me, and it makes me feel loved.

She slumps a little. "It's a Bruce Lee movie." She looks up. "You know, karate and all." Then she turns off her phone. "Ted actually likes that stuff. I wouldn't be surprised if Adam does too. It's a boy thing." She stands up. "It'll be great. We'll have dinner before, at the Indian place down on Wickenden." She smiles at me. "The two of us can watch *The Princess Bride* another time."

I look at her a little mystified. "How did you know?"

"About what?"

"*The Princess Bride?*"

"What about *The Princess Bride?*"

"It's like my favorite movie!" I tell her.

"No way! Mine too!"

We smile and laugh like a couple of schoolgirls, and I feel happy for the first time since I can remember.

15

Wednesday, after work, Adam and I walk down to the restaurant together. It's still hot out, but I'm wearing the same light cotton dress that I wore to Campus Dance, so I'm not sweating too much. We talk about work on the way—one of the rats is pregnant—and it helps diffuse some of the nervous energy I'm feeling.

We get there first and take a table. I stumble for a second, moving to sit across from him but wondering if he's expecting to sit next to me.

"Are you okay?" he asks, catching me as I trip on the carpeting.

It's the first time he's touched me, and that, mixed with my embarrassment makes me blush. I'm prone to it. I'm pretty sure he noticed it this time, but he doesn't say anything.

Jen and Ted show up together too, about fifteen minutes later. Not a moment too soon. I'm starving, and the topic of Hortense the pregnant rat has long since ceased being interesting.

We eat, family style, with the boys ordering beer, and I feel an overwhelming urge for a drink. I have to excuse myself halfway through the meal just to get away from it. I'm sure Jen notices.

Leaning on the bathroom sink, I take deep breaths waiting for it to pass. There's a knock. It's a one-person unisex bathroom, tiny, and I have the door locked.

I look up, turning my face to the door. "Yeah?"

A voice through the door. "It's Jen. Let me in."

She knows, she knows, I think. *I'm a drunk and a loser.* I unlock the door and crack it open.

She slips in, closes and locks the door behind her, and turns to me, grinning that schoolgirl grin. "You're doing great!" she says. She reaches into her bag, pulls out her lipstick, looks at herself in the mirror, gently pushing into me to get a better look, and carefully freshens herself.

Turning back to me, she tells me to let the boys split the bill. "You have to be careful about that sometimes," she adds thoughtfully. "Sometimes when they pay, they think you owe them something." She's wearing knee-length shorts and a loose, pale green shirt. Cute but not threatening, and I sense that she has my back. "Not something you need to worry about with Adam, though," she adds with reassurance.

Before we leave, she looks me over and seems to want to say something but doesn't. I'm sure it's something about the way I look, and I ask her if I look okay.

She smiles at me, picking up on the insecurity. "You look great!"

I don't believe her, but I'm glad to hear it anyway.

An hour later, the four of us are squeezed on a three-person couch watching Bruce Lee take on a small army of Chinese mercenaries. We're hip-to-hip, with me at the end, and I'm getting a rush feeling our legs touch. He's got on jeans, but I can still feel his warmth, and the urge to touch him and be touched finally squelches my desire for a drink.

We say goodbye to Jen and Ted after the movie and head back to Pitman Street, like we're already a couple. It's a little strange—going home together without actually *being* together, without really even knowing each other. But then part of me feels like I *do* know him, like I am completely comfortable with him, like we *are* a couple.

When we get up to our apartment, I tell him how much fun I had, and we pause outside my door for a moment. Then, in a rush, we move our faces into each other, but it's too fast, and we bang our teeth together in an audible snap. Pulling back and wincing in pain, I move my tongue over my front tooth. Not chipped . . . but tattered flesh on my upper lip . . . I can taste a little blood, but I'm okay. I look back up at him, standing there like a Roman frieze, and laugh before going in more slowly.

It's a deep kiss this time, lasting no more than a second or two, but it's *great*, strong and warm and full of passion. I pull back, step into my room, and close the door behind me. I spend the next half hour texting with Jen.

I SHOULDN'T HAVE KISSED HIM.

NO, IT WAS PERFECT.

I SHOULD HAVE SAID SOMETHING BEFORE I CLOSED THE DOOR.

NO, NO, NO! YOU DID IT JUST RIGHT!

REALLY??? I SHOULDN'T HAVE CLOSED THE DOOR ON HIM AT ALL.

EMILY, RELAX. GO TO SLEEP. IT'S ONLY WEDNESDAY!

Not wanting to go back out into the apartment, I go to sleep without even brushing my teeth. When I see him the next morning, it's like it never happened, and I feel a little like I'm back to square one.

We walk to work together, talk a little at the office, and do our work, side-by-side. And I'm not sure. Not sure about how he feels, about what might happen next, about whether to feel awkward or not. Then, at lunch, he asks me to the movies for Friday night. "Just the two of us," he adds. "We can try that new Chinese place on Meeting Street." A date. Finally. Clear and unambiguous.

I nod at him, taking a bite of my half sub, meatball this time, acting as casual as I can. "That would be great." I sound like an idiot.

But then I notice him chewing, comfortable as can be, there across from me, and I realize that it's all good. I breathe out and relax, happy to be there with him, sitting and sharing a meatball sub.

By the time Friday afternoon rolls around, I'm a wreck. A million things are playing out in my mind. What if the date doesn't go well? What if he acts like a jerk? No, I don't think he'd do that . . . But what if he's expecting things of me that I can't give?

I call Jen.

It's almost five by the time she's there, and I only have about an hour to get ready. The lab closes down at four on Friday, but Adam still isn't back yet: He'd said he'd be at the

SciLi—the Science Library—doing some research for a paper he's working on for Sinclair.

When she opens the door, Jen gives me that look again. "What are you wearing tonight?" she asks.

"I don't know," I pause. "I don't really have anything," I tell her, standing there in shorts and a t-shirt.

She takes me by the hand, and leads me into her room. "Come on."

I was sort of hoping she'd be able to help me out. I don't really have much in the way of clothes—especially date clothes—and right now, I can't afford anything.

She opens her closet and starts flipping through. She doesn't have that much either, but I can see that what's there is nicer than what's in my closet. Of course, she's taller and thinner than I am, but there should be *something. I hope.*

She throws a few things on the bed. Jeans, a couple of skirts, and two or three tops. I can't get the jeans over my hips.

"I've been dieting, but I'm still too fat," I tell her.

"Nonsense," she tells me back. "Adam likes you just the way you are."

Pulling the jeans off, I give her a look. "How do you know that?"

She rolls her eyes and holds a summer dress up in front of me. "Because he told me."

I'm surprised, but maybe I shouldn't be. They're room-mates; I guess they talk. I guess he told her. I feel a blanket of happiness come over me. He likes me.

She takes the dress away. "Too skimpy," she explains, pulling a jeans skirt and sizing that up next. It seems to sat-isfy her better. "Try this."

I jiggle into it. It's tight, but it may be the best I'm going to do.

She hands me a red top. I slip into it. It fits perfectly.

"You look great," she says, and I think she means it.

"I'm not sure I can sit," I tell her, turning and plopping my butt on her bed.

"Perfect," she says, looking at me seated on her covers.

It's definitely tight, definitely a bit uncomfortable, and I'm getting visions of that *I Love Lucy* episode, where she has to drive home standing up, because her skirt is so tight, and then the whole seam tears open. It makes me laugh, and I tell Jen, and she starts laughing too.

"Well don't worry, denim's pretty strong." She looks at me with a wry expression. "That skirt's tight on me too. I couldn't even get into it at one point." She wrinkles her nose. "I guess I told you, I had kind of a bad freshman year."

She seems to know just what to say to make me feel good. I still need shoes, but I get up and step over to her mirror to check myself out. *A little hippy, but it'll have to do*, I think, staring at myself in the mirror. But the length is actually perfect, just above the knee, and there's no annoying slit. I hate that.

She gives me a pair of boots, very cute, but they're too narrow, and I finally settle on a pair of black sandals—plain but not ugly and a good fit. She helps me do my toenails in a nice shade of crimson called "Femme Fatale" that matches the top.

She chimes in with one last thing that both embarrasses me and makes me bristle. "You need some new underwear," she tells me. "You know, date underwear, something sexy."

I can't afford it, and I don't want it, and it brings me back to that night, that night in the park. I feel sick to my stomach, but I don't want to tell her. For a second, I think I might cry, but my heart hardens, and the wave of emotion takes a different turn. I bark at her. "It doesn't matter. I'm not going to be sleeping with him anytime soon." *Or anyone else.*

She sits me down and strokes my back. "It's okay, sweetie. You don't have to sleep with anyone." She hugs me, there on the bed, and I burst into tears.

I tell her I'm getting my period, and I'm emotional, even though it's not true, and she tells me I can come into her room and borrow anything anytime I want, date underwear included. I think how I would never borrow someone else's underthings but that this must be what it's like to have a sister, and I cry even more. I look over at the clock. It's almost six.

I dry my eyes, and in my vulnerable state, she tries to persuade me to put on makeup. I tell her no, but she wins in the end, convincing me to don lipstick and even a little rouge. I look at myself in the mirror again, and I have to admit she was right. I wish I could get rid of my glasses.

It's a quarter after six, and I'm ready to go. He's already fifteen minutes late, and I'm starting to worry, when he calls. He lost track of time at the library: He'll meet me at the Chinese place. He's sorry. I feel my heart being pulled, and I'm annoyed, but she tells me to let it go, and I do. "It's okay. I've seen him study for hours and completely lose track of time. It doesn't mean anything."

The trip over seems to take forever, but when he sees me walk in, his face lights up, and I know the effort was all worth it.

"You look *beautiful,*" he tells me.

When we walk home after the movie, we're holding hands, and the kiss at the door to my bedroom is longer this time and just as delicious. His hands touch my hips but only just so. When I close the door to my bedroom and he turns to walk away, I tell him to have a safe trip home, giggling, as he turns around, halfway to his room.

16

My classes start that Tuesday, and we settle into a routine after that. Cooking-in and television on Monday nights, Falafel King and a rented movie on Tuesdays, nothing special on Wednesdays, late night at the lab with pizza from Ronzio's, courtesy of the department, on Thursdays, and Chinese and a movie out on Fridays.

We run together on Saturday and Sunday, and I spend most of the rest of the weekend doing my class work. I'm taking Bio 204, Population Genetics, and 165, Biostat I. The summer students are mostly from all over, but there are a few regular-session students from Brown. I open up a little and make friends with a guy named Justin, but I don't really have any contact with anyone outside of class, except to get an assignment once or twice.

Meanwhile, I finally have some money in my account, and, when Adam's birthday comes around, I decide to buy him a gift. I go downtown and pick out a silver pen. When the salesgirl asks if I want it engraved, I tell her I'm not sure, and she asks who the gift is for. "It's for my boyfriend," I say, and I realize for the first time that I actually *have* a boyfriend. Adam.

I have the pen engraved with his initials and give it to him over dinner—burgers and fries—homemade by me, and a cake from the East Side Bakery on Wayland Avenue. He loves the pen and tries it out over cake, then we go into the living room and watch *Crouching Tiger, Hidden Dragon* on DVD.

Halfway through, we start making out, and I let him go further than ever before, touching my chest through my shirt. I know he wants more, but I stop him. "I want to get to know you better," I tell him, and he nods, laying there half on top of me.

I have one leg off the couch, there underneath, and I look up at him and stroke his hair. She told him, I realize. Jen. She told him I was fragile, that something had happened to me, she didn't know what, and he listened.

We lay there in each others' arms and watch the rest of the movie. It's beautiful, and it makes me want to learn Chinese, and I can tell that Adam is loving the fight scenes, and that makes me happy too. I end up sitting in his lap with my arms around him. I can feel him underneath me, and it surprises me.

When he kisses me outside my door, I want to tell him I'm sorry that I can't give him more right now, but he doesn't push, even though I know he wants it.

"Thanks for a great birthday," he says.

A gentleman. Something I'm not used to. I smile, telling him "Goodnight" before closing the door. I know it can't last forever like this, but I savor the evening deep into the night, sleeping and dreaming of us and him and dinner-in and birthday cake, until the sun wakes me.

17

Fall closes in, and my summer classes end. In the middle of my biostat final, my mind goes blank, and I have a moment of panic before regaining my composure. It worries me, but I get A's in both classes, and Adam and I go to Boston for the day to celebrate. He buys me a static discharge toy and a book about the sun from the science museum, and we have dinner at Legal's Seafood.

I'm down to 122 lbs, 33-26-36½, and my pants are actually loose. I've been borrowing Jen's clothes—they fit pretty well now—and feel better than I have in a while. I had one bad period, one of my worst, a few weeks ago, and had to stay out sick for a couple of days, but I haven't had a drink since that night at my dad's house. All in all, pretty good. I still crave it and want to tell him, but I don't dare.

When the regular students return, and classes start back up again, Professor Sinclair invites us to their apartment for a back-to-school get-together. I finally get to meet some other students from my new department, and I actually enjoy it, reconnecting with Justin, my friend from Biostat I.

Professor Sinclair tells me I look great, and Professor Marsden is noticeably glad to see me. Adam and I are dating openly now, and they both seem happy to see us together as a couple.

We run together everyday now, and I'm fine with him seeing me in shorts. I even started going to the gym once a week to lift weights, even though my upper body is ridiculously weak.

The school year breaks up our routine a bit—more time in class, less time in the lab—but Sinclair asks me to help on a new article she's working on, about the effects of colored light on mammalian circadian rhythms, even offering to put me on as a named author.

One day, on the way back from the SciLi carrying a bunch of papers to read for the new article, someone grabs my ass, both hands, and I jerk my body around, dropping my papers and letting out a scream. It's Adam.

"You scared the shit out of me!" I yell, far more relieved than angry.

"You just look so good in those dancing jeans," he says, grinning, horny, and wanting it.

I take a deep breath, and I know it's time. No, not right now, not today, but soon. Or I'll lose him. Or I'll lose myself.

I've talked with Jen about this. I didn't tell her most of it, just that I was with someone when I really didn't want to be, and now I'm really careful. I'm sure she knew there was a lot more to it than that, but she didn't pry. She told me it was fine to take it slowly, but it wasn't fine to shut myself in and not live my life because of something someone did to me a long time ago. She was right, and I knew it.

Back at the apartment, I tell Adam—not about the past but about the fact that I'm ready.

"I thought maybe we'd go to the football game on Saturday," I start. I hate football, but I know how much he likes it, and a bunch of people from the department are going, so I figure it'll be a nice way to start the evening. We can go have dinner alone afterwards and head back to the apartment later.

"I thought you hated football."

"No," I lie. "It's just a little dull. Probably because I don't really know the rules." I can't believe how stupid I sound, and he gives me a sarcastic look. "Justin and some of the people from the department are going, and I thought it would be fun."

"Justin?"

And all of the sudden the conversation has veered off course, way off course. I don't think I've ever seen him jealous before.

I smile at him, lean in and kiss him gently. "I'm not interested in Justin. I'm interested in you." I kiss him again. "And what we can do afterwards." I'm tempted to squeeze his butt, but I can't bring myself to do it.

I don't need to. At this point, he's grinning so wide, he looks like a kid.

The football game is more fun than I had imagined (I'd gone once before, with a group, when I was a freshman, and hated it). Brown loses 14-7 to Harvard on a touchdown late in the fourth quarter. Adam explained every move along the way, although I still don't really get why a touchdown is six points.

We go back to the Chinese restaurant after that, finally shaking the last of the crowd. It's cold out, and I'm wearing blue tights under a short navy skirt, pleated. With a navy button-down sweater and black flats, it makes for a cute outfit. Not super-sexy, maybe, but it shows off my legs, which are actually looking pretty good with all the running.

Still, it's not warm enough, and I snuggle into him on the walk over, his hand on my hip. Everything is going great until he decides to order a bottle of wine with dinner.

"I told you, I don't drink," I say to him, a little too sharp, and the mood shifts.

"Well then don't have any," he says.

We argue about it, and just like that, the mood is ruined. I guess I'm not really ready after all.

We walk home in silence, me shivering with my hands under my armpits, and him, seemingly fine without even a jacket.

I say goodnight, forcing a smile but not even kissing him before disappearing into my room. He knocks and I crack the door open. I can see that he doesn't know what to say, and I feel bad.

"I'm sorry, it's my fault," I tell him. I still don't want to kiss him.

"It's okay," he says, pushing out a forced smile of his own.

When I close the door the second time, I let out a sigh. It'll be alright, I think to myself. It'll happen when the time is right. Or it won't. Either way.

I get undressed and get into my pajamas, but it's still early, and I don't feel like going to sleep. I go into the bathroom and wash out my pantyhose in the sink, hanging them over the shower rail when I'm done.

Noticing the door to his bedroom cracked open, I peek inside and catch him lying on his bed bare-chested. He's skinny and pale and very white, without a scrap of hair on his body, but he's definitely cute lying there reading. He looks up at me, and I smile at him, walking over to where he is. The room is barely-lit, and I wonder how he can see.

"How can you read like this in the dark?" I ask, standing over him.

Looking up at me, he reaches around my hip and pulls me down into him. We kiss furiously, touching each other and moving over the bed. His hands ply my body, and I finally, unambiguously, cleanly, clearly want him. I help him take my top off, and he rubs my breast through my bra. He takes his pants off, and it scares me a little, but there's no turning back, and I do the same.

We make out like that for a while, until he pulls back to tell me something. "I'm a virgin."

No shit, I think to myself.

"It doesn't matter," I tell him. "I don't have much experience myself," I add, then immediately regret saying it, but he's on to something else.

He touches my stomach, playing with my belly button and touching my panties, making me giggle and relax and want him all at the same time, until he spits it out. "I have to go to the bathroom," he says finally.

"Well hurry up!" I tell him, and he jumps out of bed and goes through the door, closing it behind him.

Taking a deep breath, I take off my bra and slip out of my panties, sliding under the covers and pulling them up to my neck. I'm naked, I think to myself. In Adam's bed. And I'm not even drunk.

I look around the room, waiting. It's a big blur, and, getting impatient, I put my glasses back on. My room is nicer, I think to myself, my heart beginning to race again. I notice a box of condoms on his nightstand next to a receipt from CVS. The last time I was in that CVS was the night of the dean's cocktail party. I won't think about it, that night in the park. It's in the past. I open the box and get a condom ready.

I still hear him fussing in the bathroom. It feels like it's taking him forever, but I calm myself. Until I check the clock and notice that another five minutes have passed. And it's gotten completely quiet. I call out for him and then again, but there's no answer.

I want to get up and take a look, but I'm naked. There's something wrong. Or is there? Did he fall asleep? Finally, I get out of bed. I think to put my pajamas back on, but I spot a bathrobe. It's blue, like mine, and I put it on and step gingerly over to the bathroom door and open it.

White. Tile. The shower. Didn't I hang my stockings over the curtain rail? I turn my head left and see them tied in a knot, dark blue, contrasting with his white skin. His tongue is bulged out. Eyes bulged too. The knot is tight around his neck, and his face is purple. Dead.

I back out through the door into the bedroom. I'm not sure how fast I'm moving, stepping backwards, wanting to get away as fast as possible, until I hit the bed and fall on the covers, spraddle-legged, my robe opening in the process.

I've lost my glasses in the fall, but I can see a blurry figure coming at me. I scurry along the quilt, but he's there on the bed in an instant, hanging over me, flat on my back, legs apart.

I can only see his outline, fuzzy, against the light. Wild hair, dark on white, and I know. Willie, the caretaker. It's quiet, the only sound being the hard breathing through flared nostrils. And I know that now too. The phone calls. Willie.

Seeing him over me, open like that, now sober, I finally remember. That night, in the park, laughing with Danny in a drunken stupor, opening my legs, pushing my underwear aside and letting him enter me in a wild frenzy. And, at that moment of climax, someone else, choking him from behind with the only thing available, strong, flesh-colored nylon. And I watched, too drunk to move, too drunk to care. When it was over, he was kneeling over me, just like he is now, and he pushed himself inside me.

I'm sober this time, and I pull back and swing at him with my arms. He grabs them with one hand and slaps me hard, giving it back to me the way I did to him that day in the supply room. He goes to do it again, but I barrel my head into his chest, grabbing him in a weird embrace until we tumble off the bed. I step over him, going for the door, but he grabs my ankle and I fall, grabbing the edge of the dresser and pulling down a glass and the copy of today's *Brown Daily Herald*.

It's then that I see another student's face plastered on the front, under the headline, missing, like Tim, the semester before. Steve. Steve! I know now for sure. Willie. He killed them. He killed them all. I kick back, hitting him in the forehead, and his grip around my ankle loosens. I'm through the door, screaming for help, pulling open the front door to the apartment, with him a step behind me, dragging me down again at the head of the stairs.

He's grabbing me, going for my neck, and I scratch his face and turn over onto my stomach with him on top of me. Feet, coming up the stairs, running. Finally, I see them and recognize the boots. Jen. She's yelling now too. And other noise. More students, people from the other apartments. One guy, big. A football player I recognize from the game, tearing him off me, and three more guys pinning him down, flailing like an animal. "It's over, it's over," I say, sitting on the ground, burying my head between my knees.

Epilogue

I didn't want to see anyone after that. I was too ashamed to even see my father. It all came out. About that night. My drinking. I was charged with obstruction of justice, fleeing the scene of a crime, failing to report a crime, tampering with evidence, and destroying evidence. I got a six month sentence at the State Women's Prison in Woonsocket. I could have fought it, but I deserved what I got. Adam was dead. Steve was dead. Even Tim. And Danny.

They sent Willie back to Indiana, to the State Hospital for the Criminally Insane. He didn't have anything to say that I wanted to hear, and I refused to even let the public defender tell me. The public defender. It had come to that.

The thing was, no one even *tried* to come see me, except my father. Nobody else. Not Jen, though I'm not sure I blame her. Not even my mother.

Then, about a month into my sentence, I have a visitor. Diane Sinclair. She smiles when she sees me. It's just a little up-curve of the lips, but it sets me at ease, there on the other side of the Plexiglas divide. We talk through the headset.

"Hi," I say, like a little girl.

"How are you doing in here?" she asks with genuine concern.

"Okay, considering."

"Considering what?" she asks, concerned, like there's something even more terrible I'm going to tell her.

Considering I have to shower and use the toilet in front of like fifty women; that I get punched in the boobs or have them squeezed until they turn purple if I don't let some gorilla in a jumpsuit cut in front of me in line; that my boyfriend is dead; that I'm never going to graduate . . .

But I don't say any of it. I just wave my hand, gesturing at the inside of my cage, and she gets it.

"Well let me know if you need anything," she says.

I nod and look at her. I'm not crying, but I can see my pleading eyes reflected in her own. "What am I going to do?"

She grimaces at me.

"I mean, I'm not even going to get my degree now." Maybe it seems selfish, and maybe I shouldn't have said it, but I'm glad I did.

"You know, I spoke to the dean. I think we can get you re-admitted. Maybe even for the summer term."

I look at her, surprised.

"You know Brown, politically correct and all. You *were* raped. And you *do* have an addiction problem."

I look down and nod.

"You'll have to go to AA," she tells me.

I would do almost anything for a drink right now. But that would be a bad idea. The worst. Not that it's even an option in here. I nod again. It's something I should have done a long time ago.

"Bill sends his love," she tells me. *Professor Marsden.* "He was going to come, but we decided it would be better if it was just me."

"Yeah," I say, reaching up and putting my hand on the glass, wanting desperately to touch her, another human being, someone who cared enough to make the effort.

The next morning, when I wake up with the sun in my eyes, I think about that morning looking at the sun through the telescope at the observatory, seeing that solar flare, and feeling the heat. This isn't over, I tell myself. Not by a long shot.

To see our other great titles,
visit us at:

BLACKBIRD BOOKS
www.bbirdbooks.com

www.ingramcontent.com/pod-product-compliance
Lightning Source LLC
Chambersburg PA
CBHW051846170626
46807CB00003B/1379